JENNY ALEXANDER

How to Get the FAMILY YOU WANT

BY

Peony Pinker

A & C Black • London

How to Get the Family You Want
by Peony Pinker

First published 2011 by
A & C Black
an imprint of Bloomsbury Publishing Plc
50 Bedford Square, London, WC1B 3DP

www.bloomsbury.com
www.jennyalexander.co.uk

ISBN 978-1-4081-3286-9

A CIP catalogue for this book is available from the British Library.

This book is produced using paper that is made from wood
grown in managed, sustainable forests. It is natural, renewable and
recyclable.The logging and manufacturing processes conform
to the environmental regulations of the country of origin.

Printed and Bound by CPI Group (UK) Ltd, Croydon CR0 4YY

3 5 7 9 10 8 6 4 2

Contents

Chapter 1
Beans for Tea and World War Three

You know when your parents are being really annoying such as, for example, when your mum is starting up her own business called 'Garden Angels' and your dad's supposed to be doing more around the house, but isn't?

And they argue all the time until you can't stand another minute of it so you just have to get out of there and take a long walk on the beach with your sister's boyfriend's dog?

Well, that's what happened to me the day that Gran was coming to visit.

It was a Friday so Dad wasn't working. He takes Thursdays and Fridays off because he's a sports reporter on the Three Towns Gazette, which means he has to work weekends, going to cricket matches and stuff. Nice work if you can get it, Mum says.

Anyway, as he was at home all day and she was out mowing lawns and hacking hedges, Mum had left him a list of chores such as 'tidy house', 'buy food' and 'prepare evening meal'. Judging by the state of the kitchen when me and Primrose got home from school, he hadn't done any of them.

The kitchen takes up the whole of the ground floor of our house, so it's got both the front door and the back door going out of it. A third door leads to the stairs up to the sitting-room; then above that is my bedroom and Primrose's. Mum and Dad's bedroom and Dad's study are right at the top of the house. All the houses in Harbour Row are very tall and thin.

The back door was open and the sound of snoring was wafting in from the yard. We looked out and saw Dad snoozing on a sun-lounger with his newspaper spread across his belly like a blanket.

'Dad!' Primrose woke him up.

He shifted under his newspaper and a few pages slid onto the ground.

'W-what time is it?' he mumbled, rubbing his eyes.

Instead of answering, she handed him Mum's list. He groaned. Then, true to his motto, 'If a job's worth doing it's worth getting someone else to do it,' he said, 'You'll have to help me, girls.'

Primrose laughed. 'Sorry, Dad. I've got revision to do!'

Once you get past Year 9 you can use exams as an excuse for getting out of anything you don't want to do for the whole summer term. I learnt that from Primrose. You don't actually have to do any revision – Dad and me both knew perfectly well that Primrose was going to spend the next half hour trying on every single thing in her wardrobe and doing her make-up before Matt came round.

She flounced off upstairs to get changed and Dad looked at me. I didn't see why I should have to help if Primrose wasn't going to, and anyway, as I pointed out to him, the list clearly said 'Dave' at the top, not 'Dave, Primrose and Peony'.

'You've got plenty of time,' I said. 'Mum won't be home for ages.'

'Fair enough,' goes Dad in a you-can't-blame-a-bloke-for-trying kind of way.

Mum had been working late every night for weeks. She and her friend Stella were trying to do as much lawn-mowing and weeding as possible so they could build a big list of customers. Then in the winter-time when everything stopped growing, those people might think of them for winter jobs like making ponds and digging vegetable patches.

Unfortunately for Dad, I was wrong about him having plenty of time because Mum decided to stop work early that day in honour of Gran's visit. When she walked in, all covered in bits of grass and dust, he was just cramming the odds and ends that had been left lying around on the surfaces into the space at the front of the food cupboard – which should have been full of food if he had done the shopping.

'This place looks like a pigsty!' Mum said, stamping the dirt off her feet on the doormat. 'What on earth have you been doing all day?'

'I've been tidying,' Dad said indignantly. He pointed to the list. 'Item number one!'

'Your mother will be here any minute and you haven't even tidied up?'

'Well, see, the thing is, Jan, my mum doesn't mind a bit of mess.'

Mum stopped undoing her boot laces and stepped deliberately off the mat. She clomped across to the sink to get a glass of water, leaving a trail of grass cuttings and dirt all over the floor.

'All right, Dave, tell me this – what have you bought for supper tonight? Or does your mum not mind a bit of going hungry either?'

'No-one will be going hungry,' Dad assured her. 'I'm thinking, beans on toast!'

Dad's cooking skills didn't stretch much further than beans, pizza, pasta and take-away, and that was pretty much all we'd been living on since Mum started her gardening business. When she told him we weren't getting enough vegetables he invented 'beans 'n greens' by putting a lettuce leaf on top. When she said we needed fruit in our diet he sprinkled our spaghetti with sultanas.

To be honest, Primrose and me preferred Dad's cooking. It was great. I mean, you could rely on him never to spring yucky things on you such as gooseberries, rhubarb, spinach or cauliflower. But it really annoyed Mum.

'I know you've raised laziness to a fine art, but surely you could make an effort when your mother's coming!' she thundered.

Dad pointed out that it was his day off, and as far as he was aware normal people regarded a day off as time to stop working and relax.

11

'What's that supposed to mean – normal people?' goes Mum.

'It means I liked you better before you went workaholic!'

'Well pardon me for not being consistent like you. You've always been a waste of space!'

Primrose swept in looking for her eye-pencil. She would never have guessed where it was so I pointed to the food cupboard for her.

'Thanks, Peony,' she said, opening the door. A blue biro and a bunch of old bus tickets fell out. She shoved them back in again. 'What's with all the shouting? It's like World War Three in here!'

That's exactly what Mum and Dad say when me and Primrose are arguing but you could tell it wasn't a good idea saying it to them. They straight away stopped shouting at each other and turned on Primrose.

'If it's like World War Three in here that's because the place looks like a bomb hit it!' Mum said. 'We all know your father's a lazy slob...'

Dad looked as if he might protest but then thought the better of it. He didn't really have a leg to stand on.

'...but that doesn't mean you have to copy him! When was the last time you did anything around the house?'

'Well, I'm sorry but I can't help at the moment,'

Primrose said smugly. 'I've got revision.'

'Then you won't be needing this,' goes Mum, swiping the eye-pencil out of her hand.

It was like flicking a switch. Primrose is the only person I know who can go from smug to stroppy in two seconds flat.

'That's mine!' she said. 'Give it back!'

'You'll have it back when you've helped with the tidying-up,' goes Mum.

Primrose glanced at the clock. Matt would be here any minute and she hadn't finished her make-up. Mum said if she was feeling so stressed about her revision maybe she shouldn't be seeing Matt every single day after school.

Right on cue, we heard him coming up the front steps. Primrose snatched her eye-pencil in panic but it was too late. Matt tapped on the open door and walked in. Old Sam, who usually trots in first, was dragging behind. Dogs can always sense danger. I ran and stroked him so he wouldn't be scared. When Primrose is kicking off, wolves and lions would run for cover.

'Everything OK?' said Matt. He was probably wishing he had been able to sense danger too. Then he would have reached our house and gone right on walking.

'You won't believe this!' blurted Primrose. 'Mum wants us to stop seeing each other!'

'She didn't exactly say that,' Dad pointed out. 'She said maybe you could see a bit less of each other during the exam period because then you'd have more time for revising.'

'And for pulling your weight around the house,' added Mum.

'That's all you care about, the rotten house!' cried Primrose. 'You don't care about me! When I fail everything and drop out of school and end up living in a cardboard box you'll be happy because at least I did my share of the hoovering!'

She looked at Matt, expecting him to back her up, but he didn't meet her eye. Sam gave a little whimper. I stroked his head again.

'As if I haven't got enough stress already!' wailed Primrose.

'Ahem...' Matt cleared his throat. 'Maybe your mum's got a point?' he ventured.

Was he mad? Primrose gave him a glare. Unbelievably, he carried on.

'I've got exams this term too, and my parents have told me they think I should be staying home some evenings to revise.'

They would, when you came to think about it. I mean, they spent a fortune sending him to St Cuthbert's College so they must be keen for him to do well. But none of us had seen this coming. Mum nodded approvingly. Dad glanced nervously at Primrose. Sam stuck his nose under his paw.

Primrose said, in a voice that could make a polar bear shiver, 'If that's what you think...'

She was furious, but not fiery furious. She was frosty furious, which is even worse, though Matt didn't know it yet because he'd only been going out with her for a few weeks. He had never seen her in a full-on strop.

'Can I take Sam for a walk?' I said.

I couldn't hang around and watch. I had to get out of there quick-smart or else I might just snap and say, 'Primrose, you're an idiot. Matt's the best boyfriend you've ever had and you're going to drive him away!'

Chapter 2
The Booted-out Boyfriend and the Super-selfish Sister

If all the animals in the world were to have a race, Sam would end up battling it out at the back with the sloths and snails. It's not his fault, he's just really old. Matt says in his young days he was always on the go, rounding everyone up. That's the sheep-dog in him. These days he'd have trouble rounding up a cabbage.

I let him go first down the front steps. There are eleven of them, which must be like going down

Mount Everest for him. All the houses in this part of Polgotherick have steps up to the front door because they're on a steep hill overlooking the harbour. They were built before people had cars so there aren't any roads, just zig-zag paths that wind their way up out of the town and down towards the sea.

It was drizzling but I didn't want to go back indoors and get a coat. It could be just a passing shower and anyway, like Gran says, skin is water-proof. If it wasn't, imagine what would happen when you got in the bath. Or when you were at the swimming pool with fifty billion other people – you'd all soak up the water and get jammed.

Sam finally made it to the bottom of the steps and started plodding down the path towards the sea. Because he's so old and there aren't any cars you don't have to keep him on the lead. He's also a bit blind which means he has to stop every few seconds to get his bearings by having a good sniff around.

By the time we got to the bend by the Seafarers' chapel I was beginning to feel better. That's how it works when you're walking a dog. You can be in a steaming temper when you set off but then ten minutes later you'll be watching him sniffing a chip paper and suddenly notice you aren't feeling upset any more.

Since Primrose had been going out with Matt I had been walking Sam every day and he had become like my best friend. Ideally, I'd have liked to have a dog of my own, of course. The problem was, Dad didn't like dogs. He had been scared of them ever since one bit him on the bum when he was nine.

You would have thought that having dear old Sam around might help him to get over it, but no luck so far. Still, a borrowed dog is definitely better than no dog at all. If you've got a very annoying family like me and you aren't allowed to have a dog, you really should try to find someone who will let you borrow theirs, that's what I say.

The tide was coming in. Some of the small boats in the harbour had already lifted out of the mud and were bobbing about in the shallow water. There weren't many people out and about on such a murky day, just Toby from school and his little sister Leah. They were crabbing off the end of the harbour wall. I went to see if they'd caught anything.

Toby and Leah's dad ran the Scouts troop in Polgotherick and their mum was in charge of the Guides. They were always going off on family hikes, canoeing holidays and stuff like that.

'Hey Peony,' said Toby. 'Nice weather for ducks!'

'Look at all the crabs we've got,' goes Leah. The bucket was full of big brown crabs, all crawling over each other.

'Matt's at your house then,' Toby said, nodding towards Sam. Then he looked up at me and said, 'What's wrong?'

I shrugged. Same old, same old. Primrose kicking off. Mum and Dad arguing.

They never used to be this bad. Before Mum started her business they had their ups and downs like everyone else. Mum sometimes got annoyed when Dad was being a slacker, but most of the time she liked his laid-back ways. Dad sometimes got fed up with Mum whizzing around like a whirlwind, but most of the time he admired the way she got things done.

'Mum's off the scale with work,' I said, 'so Dad's gone off the scale with slacking, and all they do is argue all the time.'

Toby didn't know what to say. If you needed someone to get a stone out of your horse's hoof or make a stretcher out of sweatshirts or build a shelter from sticks and leaves, Toby was the one to ask. But he wasn't a great one for talking about things.

'If you want to get out of the house you can always come to ours,' he said. 'We're digging up that hedgehog we found on the top road a few weeks ago to see if we can find the bones.'

It was a tempting offer but I told him my Gran was coming later. Then all of a sudden, it started bucketing down so Toby and Leah tipped their crabs back over the edge and sprinted off towards their house. Sam and me went trudging back up the hill.

We were both soaked by the time we turned the last bend and came in sight of Harbour Row. Matt was walking down the path towards us. He did not look happy. I thought maybe he was cross with me for keeping Sam out in the rain in case he got a chill or something, but as we got closer I just knew that wasn't it.

'She's dumped me!' he blurted out. 'Everything seemed to be going so well. I just don't understand it.'

Blooming Primrose – I knew this was going to happen!

'What did she say?'

'She said, if I wasn't going to stick up for her in her most stressful time, what with exams and everything, then as far as she was concerned it was over.'

'And what did you say?'

'Well, I said all right then. I didn't want to make her feel even more stressed by arguing.'

I rolled my eyes.

'That's not what you're supposed to say. You're supposed to plead.'

'W-what?'

'You plead and then she takes you back.'

It was raining so hard we might as well have been standing under a cold shower. I grabbed Matt's arm and pulled him towards the house.

'I'm not going back in there!' he said.

The shed under the front steps wasn't locked. I opened the door and we dived inside. Sam stood out on the path looking bedraggled until Matt scooped him up and sat him on the floor between our feet.

'Look, this is the way it works,' I said. 'Primrose is a bit of a drama queen.'

Actually, she's a lot more than a bit of a drama queen, she's one hundred per cent of one, but I didn't want to completely put him off.

'She's like this with everyone. She gets in a strop and makes a big scene, then it all blows over and everything's great again. Trust me.'

She must have dumped her last boyfriend, Mushy Marcus, a dozen times but he always came back, and then they were even more mushy with each other than before. Until Marcus eventually got fed up with it and Primrose went into her mega-mooch, but I didn't even want to think about that.

21

'You weren't there,' Matt said, gloomily. 'She wasn't messing around.'

Then he picked Sam up and stepped outside.

'Goodbye, Peony.'

They walked away up the zig-zag path.

'Can I still see Sam?' I called after him, but I don't think he heard me through the rain. And anyway, what was I thinking? Of course I wouldn't see Sam if Matt stopped coming to see Primrose.

I was as mad as a wasp in a bottle. I already had Mum and Dad arguing all the time and now Primrose would be a complete pain like she always was when her love-life took a dive. To make matters worse, I would have to get through it all without even having Sam to cheer me up. What about *my* most stressful time?

If there was a Most Selfish Sister competition, Primrose would win it hands down.

Chapter 3
The Silver Surfer and the Happy Haddock

I stayed in my bedroom until I heard Gran arrive, and luckily Primrose stayed in hers. I didn't even want to look at her. As soon as I went into the kitchen I could see that Mum and Dad were at the not-wanting-to-even-look-at-each-other stage too.

Gran was as brown as a nut. She was wearing her usual shorts and sandals, and a new purple and green top like the ones you see hanging outside the beach shop in the breeze.

'Cup of tea, Gwen?'

Mum put the kettle on while Gran was giving me a hug. Primrose came down and Gran tried to hug her too but she was as limp as last week's lettuce in her arms because of the trauma of breaking up with Matt. Gran didn't ask.

Mum opened the cupboard to get some tea-bags and the blue biro fell out again, along with the bunch of old bus tickets, some empty envelopes and half a packet of chewing gum. Mum gave Dad a dirty look, scooped the whole lot up and dumped it in the bin. Dad pretended not to notice.

'How's the surf in St Ives?' he asked Gran.

Gran took up surfing eight years ago, after she and Grandpa split up. She got so into it she moved to St Ives, which is like Polgotherick but with waves. Then she had the great idea of becoming a surfing instructor. Gran has lots of great ideas and nearly all of them turn out to be terrible, but this one proved to be a winner.

It seems that heaps of old people wish they could surf but think they're too old to learn. When they see my Gran out there in her wetsuit they decide maybe they aren't. She must be the oldest surfing instructor in the universe but she still brings the customers in. She's quite famous in St Ives – they call her the Silver Surfer.

Mum opened the fridge door to get some milk and found there wasn't any. 'Sorry,' she said to Gran. 'It looks like tea's off because we don't seem to have any milk in the house. Dave must have been so busy all day that he simply could not find ten minutes to do some food shopping.'

'That's OK,' Gran said. 'I often drink my tea black.'

Dad was pleased with that answer. Mum wasn't. 'It'll be beans on toast for supper too. Same reason,' she said.

'No worries,' goes Gran. 'As it happens I've booked a table for us all at the Happy Haddock tonight. My treat.'

'What a good job I didn't prepare anything then!' said Dad, really pushing his luck. Mum looked as if she might explode.

In the nick of time, explosion-wise, there was a rat-a-tat-tat on the door and Mr Kaminski came in.

'Hello, hello,' he said. 'I needing help. Is good time, yes?'

'Yes!' we all said at once.

Gran introduced herself. 'I'm Gwen, Dave's mother. Primrose and Peony's grandmother.'

'Viktor Kaminski. I living next door.'

'I would offer you some tea if we had any milk,' said Mum. 'I left Dave a list but it seems...'

'You wanted some help, Viktor?' asked Dad, cutting Mum off, much to everyone's relief.

Mr Kaminski explained that he had run into some difficulties with the problem page. Dad should have been doing it really, because his editor had asked him to take over when the real agony aunt, Daphne, went missing. But it turned out Dad was completely clueless, and Mr Kaminski had taken pity on him and offered to help.

Before long, Mr Kaminski was doing it on his own, taking the letters, writing the answers and giving them to Dad. All Dad had to do was correct his English and send it to his editor.

Mr Kaminski said he didn't want any payment because he enjoyed doing it, so Dad bought him presents instead. As Dad wasn't very adventurous on the presents front, Mr K was building up quite a collection of cardigans.

'Is summer holiday coming,' said Mr Kaminski. 'Many letters about family things. What can I do with childrens when not going to school? Such things I do not know. I have no childrens, never, just me and my wife.'

He got that sad look he always gets when he mentions his wife because he still misses her.

He shook himself as if he had to literally shake it off. Then he pulled a handful of letters out of his cardigan pocket and unfolded them. Dad reached over and took one off the top.

'Dear Daphne,' he read out loud. 'My children argue all the time and with the long school holidays coming up, my husband says if we have another summer like last year he's putting them both up for adoption...'

'She should make their waste-of-space father get up off his sun-lounger and organise some activities for them,' suggested Mum.

'Or,' said Dad, 'maybe she should stop working all the hours and spend some time at home for a change.'

Mr Kaminski, who had got out his pencil to take some notes, slid it back into his pocket again. Gran asked Dad to read us a bit more of the letter.

'Dear Daphne...my children...blah blah, etc... adoption...' He found where he was up to and read the next line. 'I try to keep them apart but they seem to seek each other out. It's as if they actually want to argue. What can I do? From a frantic mum.'

'They should get rid of the annoying younger child,' said Primrose. 'Farm her out to an auntie or something. Then she can't keep winding her sister up.'

'Don't be stupid,' I said. 'They should get rid of the older one because she's probably a drama queen.'

Primrose went purple. 'Did you hear that? She called me a drama queen – me! As if I haven't got enough to cope with! Today of all days!'

She did her very best tragic hero look. Mr Kaminski glanced longingly at the door. He was obviously starting to realise he had come to the wrong place for advice about family life.

Gran said, 'She needs to stop trying to keep them apart and make the whole family spend more time together.'

We all gawped at her.

'They'll kill each other,' said Mum. 'Which would be an even bigger problem for the problem page.'

Gran said surely we had heard the old saying, 'The family that plays together stays together'?

'Put that in your answer,' she told Mr Kaminski.

Dad said on the contrary, it should be 'The family that plays together falls out over the rules.'

'Look what happens whenever we try to play Monopoly,' he said. Which pretty much proved his point.

Mr Kaminski looked confused. 'I go now,' he muttered. 'I see you very busy.'

Gran reached across the table to shake his hand.

'It's been a delight to meet you, Viktor,' she said.

It's hard to tell with old people, but I could have sworn he blushed.

Gran asked me to walk down to the Happy Haddock with her and help her get settled in. When we were little, she used to sleep in my room and I would move in with Primrose, but now we were older she said it was easier for everyone if she stayed at the pub.

Dad carried her bags down the front steps. Then I took the little one and she took the big one and we wheeled them down the path towards the harbour. It wasn't raining any more but you could feel there was more rain on the way so I was wearing my coat this time – one soaking in a day is more than enough.

'You haven't really booked a table, have you Gran?' I asked.

She laughed, and shook her head.

'No – fingers crossed they're not completely booked!'

Chapter 4
The Wise Old Owl and the Wishes that Won't Work

Gran asked me how I was getting on at school, which was really nice considering no-one else seemed to bother lately.

'School's all right,' I said. 'But Mum and Dad keep arguing and Primrose is being a proper pain.'

Gran put her free arm round me. She said everyone's mum and dad argued sometimes and everyone's big sister could be a pain. It was just a bad patch we were going through and it would soon pass.

'Things will settle down once your mum's got her business up and running,' she said.

I nearly asked if I could go and live in St Ives with her in the meantime, but the problem with Gran is she's unpredictable. One minute you might be having a normal life, going to school and everything, and the next minute she could be whisking you off to live on a bus and sell beads.

'I'm an ideas person,' that's what Gran always says. The trouble is she gets all these ideas and goes for them without really thinking things through.

When she and Grandpa lived in Polgotherick, Gran got the idea they should turn their house into a bed-and-breakfast. But she had forgotten she isn't really a morning person and she could never get up in time to cook breakfast for the guests. Grandpa had to do it, which was a disaster because he burnt everything – bacon, sausages, even scrambled eggs. That must be where Dad gets his barbecuing skills from.

Gran's B&B got zero stars in the Polgotherick guide the next year but by that time it didn't matter any more because she had decided they should up sticks and live in Spain, which is a whole nother story.

'Tell me about Mr Kaminski,' Gran said, as we hit the puddle-zone at the bottom of the hill. You don't get puddles on the zig-zag paths because they're too steep. When it rains hard you get rivers.

'He used to be a sea captain,' I told her. 'He's been right round the world.'

'That's interesting...what else?'

I thought about it.

'He knows things. He's like a wise old owl.'

'I like owls,' said Gran.

The tide was right in now and all the boats were bobbing in the harbour. We stopped to look at them.

'What sort of things does Mr Kaminski know?' asked Gran.

'Things like how to get what you want.'

I told her about Mr Kaminski's method – you had to be exact, you had to work out exactly what you wanted, and then you had to write it down. You had to think and think about it until you could see a way you might be able to get it. If you tried and your first idea didn't work you just had to think again.

'We all did it,' I said. 'I wanted Primrose to stop hanging out with this horrible girl called Bianca because she was being really mean to me after school. Primrose wanted to be called Annabel.

32

Dad wanted not to have to write the problem page and Mum wanted to stop working at the Green Fingers Garden Centre but still work with plants.'

The amazing thing was, it worked! That was why I had another list of exact wishes in my pocket right now that I had written while I was drying off in my bedroom after my last *ever* – thanks to Primrose – walk with Sam.

We got to the Happy Haddock and went in. It was one of the oldest buildings in Polgotherick, right at the end of the harbour, overlooking the sea. Inside, it was dark like a cave even on sunny days, and nets of tiny twinkling lights hung from the black ceiling beams. It always smelt of chips and old chairs.

'Gwen! Good to see you again!'

Jane, the owner, used to go to school with Gran a thousand years ago. She squeezed herself out from behind the bar and gave her a hug. 'I've put you in number 4 as we aren't busy this weekend.'

'The best room in the house,' goes Gran. 'I'm honoured! And can I book a table for five tonight?'

We took the bags up to Gran's room. It was the one at the front with the big bow window. Gran flopped down on the bed.

'Are you going to show me this list then, or is it secret?' she asked.

I don't keep any secrets from Gran, so I handed it over. The list said, 'I want Primrose to stop being a drama queen. I want Dad to stop being lazy and I want Mum to stop being so one-track on work, because then they won't argue all the time.'

Gran looked at my list for a while, not saying anything. Then she patted the bed beside her for me to sit down.

'See, here's the thing, Peony,' she said. 'Mr Kaminski's method is brilliant. It's the best possible way to try and get what you want. But there's one kind of wish that won't come true, and that is wanting to change other people.

'Take your dad, for example,' she said. 'He was born lazy. It's in his nature. Trying to make him stop being lazy would be like trying to make a lion stop lying around in the sun all day and leap around in the trees like a lively little monkey.'

She said Mum was naturally a hard worker. She loved to be busy! Trying to make someone like Mum stop throwing herself into her work would be like trying to make a busy bee stop buzzing around and sit stone still like a frog all day, waiting for a fly.

And as for trying to make Primrose stop being a drama queen, you'd have a better chance of

34

turning a preening peacock into a plain little hedge sparrow.

'It can't be done,' said Gran. 'But don't look so glum!' She gave me a hug. Her skin smelt of coconut sun cream.

Gran said that on the whole it didn't matter if you couldn't change people because you could always choose who you hung around with. You could decide to keep away from the ones you didn't like, such as Bianca, and hang out with the ones you did. Except for family.

'You can't choose your family,' Gran went on. 'So since you can't have the family you want, the trick is to learn to want the family you've got.'

I must have looked gloomy again because Gran gave me another hug.

'That's never going to happen,' I said.

'Never say "never", Peony!'

Gran jumped up and started unpacking her things.

'A family is like a pack of pets. All different kinds can live together perfectly happily but they're never going to learn to get along if you keep them in separate pens. What you all need is a project to bring you together.'

I didn't like to mention what happened when she and Grandpa got the joint project of retiring to Spain after they sold the B&B. They went out there together, and she came back on her own. He was still living there with Juanita.

I was beginning to wish I hadn't told her about my list but it was too late. She had already got her thinking-cap on. I guess it's just her nature. Trying to change her would be like trying to make a crafty rat leave a lovely lump of cheese in the middle of a maze and not try to work out how to get to it.

'Don't you worry about this!' she said. 'Leave it with me. I'm sure I'll think of something!'

Chapter 5
Gran's Great Idea and a Quick Getaway

The next day was Saturday, which is normally the best day of the week because I help out at the kennels in Hayden's Lane. I get up before everyone else and walk up the zig-zag path on my own to meet Becky, the other Saturday girl. Then we go on across the fields between her house and Hayden's Lane together.

Becky is living proof that all teenagers are not a pain like Primrose, whatever Mum says. She's thirteen and a half, which is only two years younger than Primrose, but she doesn't have moochy moods or go ballistic at the slightest thing. Or talk about make-up and boys till you wish your ears would drop off.

Unfortunately, Becky was on holiday and Mum said I couldn't walk up to the kennels on my own.

'Your father will walk up with you.'

'What?' goes Dad.

'I would do it myself but I've got lots of lawns to cut before lunch.'

Dad isn't a walking kind of person so we took the car. We passed Matt coming down the hill. His family owns the kennels and he used to work there on Saturdays, but now he's seventeen he's got a proper job at the beach cafe. Becky and me always pass him in the lane on Saturday mornings. He gives us a cheery hello and jokes around.

I waved at him through the car window. He saw me and waved back, but it was a sad and sorry sort of wave, which was Primrose's fault. She had crushed him like a cornflake and now he was in bits.

Rotten Primrose! Rotten Mum for being too busy to walk up with me and rotten Dad for making us take the car on a lovely sunny morning like this! I wished I hadn't shown Gran my list. At least when I believed I might be able to change them there seemed to be some hope.

Plus now I had the extra worry that Gran might do something drastic, such as book us all on a team-building weekend where we had to rescue each other from icy rivers and stuff.

By the time I started cleaning out the pens I was already feeling grumpy, and things did not pick up. Matt's little brother, who is only nine, was doing Becky's job and Mrs Teverson still wouldn't let me walk the big boisterous dogs, even though I'm much bigger than him.

Mum picked me up at lunchtime in Stella's van, which they're using for their business. It's got grass growing in the back like a proper lawn from where earth and grass seed have spilled out of the bags. By the time we got home, Gran had arrived and Dad was cooking frozen pizza for lunch.

Primrose kept checking her phone every three seconds to see if Matt was ready to beg her forgiveness and get back together. When she wasn't checking her phone she was checking her look in the mirror in case he should turn up out of the blue with some chocs and a mushy card like Marcus used to do.

Gran didn't mention any mad plans so by the time Mum went back to work I was feeling a bit less worried, although she did wink at me over her pizza when no-one was looking. That didn't feel like a good sign.

We were clearing up the lunch things when there was a rat-a-tat at the door. 'Come in!' yelled Dad, expecting it to be one of the neighbours.

It was a man we didn't know. He had a big grey and white rabbit under his arm.

Gran jumped up to greet the man and he handed the rabbit over. Then he went back down the front steps to get 'the rest of his things'. We all watched in astonishment as he brought in a hutch, two feeding bowls, some rabbit food, a bag of hay, a box of cat litter and a litter tray.

The man shook hands with Gran and said it had been a pleasure doing business with her. Then he left and Gran said, 'This is Dennis – your new rabbit!'

Everyone looked at her as if she was one sandwich short of a picnic, and then Dad said what we were all thinking.

'We can't keep him – Jan will go mental!'

'Nonsense!' goes Gran. 'She'll love him. I mean, what's not to love?'

Dennis's fur was much softer than any dog's or cat's. His nose twitched all the time, making his whiskers jiggle, and he had the sweet fresh smell of new hay.

Gran said he was two years old and he had to live indoors because that was what he was used to. But the man had assured her he was fully house-trained. He could be relied upon to do all his pees and poos in the litter tray.

'You can put it beside his hutch in the space under the stairs.'

The space under the stairs was always crammed with stuff we couldn't be bothered to put away such as shoes and beach bags. Gran organised us as we cleared it out and installed Dennis's things. It was crazy but, as Dad always says, Gran's like a force of nature. When she gets enthusiastic about something it's no good trying to stand in her way.

Gran put Dennis down on the floor so he could investigate his new home. He hopped across to his hutch and gave it a good sniff. We had filled the bedroom end with fresh hay and covered the other end with newspaper. One bowl was full of rabbit food and the other one full of water but he didn't seem hungry because he hopped in, sniffed them, rubbed his chin on them and then hopped back out again.

He hopped around the room after that, rubbing his chin on everything as if he had the itchiest chin in the world. Then he sat under the table and started washing his nose with his paws.

'He's sweet,' Primrose said. She doesn't really like animals but Matt was animal-mad like all the Teversons, so she was probably thinking Dennis would be an added attraction when he came crawling back.

'Yes, he's nice,' agreed Dad. He was probably thinking it could have been worse – Gran could have gone out and got us a dog!

Dennis finished washing and hopped across the room. He backed up against the cupboard under the sink and did a pee. Then he dropped six little round poos beside the puddle and hopped back under the table again.

'I thought the man said...'

'You'd better pop down to the shop and get some kitchen-roll, Dave, just in case he takes a while to settle in,' said Gran. 'And perhaps it would be a good idea to buy a book about looking after rabbits from Polgotherick Pets as well.'

Dad went to the shops and Primrose disappeared upstairs to do her hair for the trillionth time. Gran and I sat on the floor with our legs stretched out in front of us. We kept very still, and eventually Dennis got brave enough to come out from under the table. He crept towards us with his body pressed low to the floor, stopping every few seconds to check we still weren't moving. Eventually he got brave enough to come right up and sniff our feet.

'I told you I would think of something,' Gran said, with a grin. 'Have you noticed it's already working?'

I gave her a quizzical look.

'You've spent two whole hours together getting Dennis settled in and you haven't argued at all. I bet you even forgot for a while just how annoying Primrose and your dad can be!'

'Yes...but what about when Mum gets home?'

The mention of Mum seemed to remind Gran that she had to be somewhere else. She was having tea with Auntie Bee.

Typical! She gets a hare-brained idea then leaves everyone else to pick up the pieces, like starting the B&B and then leaving Grandpa to cook the breakfasts.

When Gran got up, Dennis shot back under the table. After she had gone, I stayed sitting on the floor and about nine hours later he got his confidence back enough to come and sniff my legs again. Then he got really brave and hopped over my knees. The second time he did it I tried to catch him but that sent him scuttling straight back under the table.

He didn't seem that keen on making friends but that was probably just as well considering the minute Mum got home she would one hundred per cent definitely say he had to go.

Chapter 6
One Week's Trial and
Two Kinds of Poos

Primrose was taking pictures of Dennis under the table with her phone. Every time it flashed, he thumped hard on the floor with his back feet. Flash, thump! Flash, thump! Flash, thump!

'You should send one to Matt,' I suggested. 'He'd like to see Dennis.'

'I'm sure he would,' she agreed, haughtily. 'And perhaps he should have thought of that before he abandoned me in my hour of need.'

She wasn't even joking.

Dad came back with a four-pack of kitchen rolls and a little book called You and Your Rabbit. He gave it to me as Primrose was still half under the table trying to get the perfect shot. Then he stashed the kitchen rolls on top of Dennis's hutch, pulled one out, and went to clean up the pees and poos on the floor in front of the sink. There was quite a collection by then.

I flicked the pages and found a section about 'Your rabbit's noises'. Generally rabbits are silent animals, it said, but they may growl if excited and they may scream if they get really, really scared. If they feel alarmed they thump hard with their back feet to warn other rabbits of possible danger.

'Stop taking photos,' I said to Primrose. 'That thumping means you're frightening him.'

She pulled out from under the table so I could see her face and not just her bottom. 'Oh,' she said. 'I thought he was messing around.' Primrose might be a prize pain in virtually every way but you can say this for her, she isn't cruel.

As soon as she pulled out and Dennis wasn't cornered any more he hopped off towards the sink and did another pee and a bunch more poos on Dad's newly-wiped floor. Dad pursed his lips. Primrose and me laughed.

'Put him on his litter tray so he gets the right idea,' I said. 'Maybe he just can't remember where it is.'

Dad tried to pick Dennis up, but Dennis went to bite his hand and he jumped back like a pup with a jellyfish. Primrose and me laughed again, which made Dad more determined, and after a few more tries he finally got hold of Dennis and dropped him gently in his litter tray.

Dennis flicked his back feet, scattering cat litter all over the place, and hopped straight out again. Then he ducked past Dad and did few more poos on the floor in front of the sink. Primrose and me laughed so hard even Dad saw the funny side.

I looked up house-training in the book. It said when you move your rabbit to a different room he will choose his favourite place to do his pees and poos, and that's where you have to put his litter tray. Once he's using it all the time, you can edge it gradually into the place you actually want it to be.

Dad cleared up the mess and we put Dennis's litter tray on the floor in front of the sink. Dennis rubbed the edges of it with his chin and then hopped in. I looked up 'itchy chin' in the glossary and found a section called 'chinning'. It said rabbits rub their chins on things to say 'this is mine!' So maybe he really was settling in. I mean, he had claimed pretty much everything he could reach in the whole room by then, including all our feet.

Dad said he had things to do, which basically meant he was getting out of there before Dennis had a chance to do any more mess on the floor. Primrose went to get changed again because Matt would be finished at the cafe now and could therefore appear on the doorstep at any moment.

I read in the book that rabbits are nervous around new people. You had to bear in mind, it said, that almost every animal rabbits meet in the wild would probably like to eat them. So Dennis wasn't being unfriendly with all his hiding and trying to bite – he just wasn't sure about us yet.

I lay down on the floor on my back and shut my eyes. I thought that way he couldn't feel scared of me. I heard the soft sound of his furry feet as he hopped a bit nearer. I felt his whiskers on my bare foot and nearly burst into giggles.

Dennis sniffed all the way up the side of my leg, then the side of my body, then my cheek. He sniffed my ear. His huffy breath sounded really loud and I was a bit worried he might bite me. I don't know how I managed to keep still. He huffed across the top of my forehead. Then I got this really odd feeling, like a gentle tugging. He was nibbling my hair!

Suddenly the front door opened. Dennis shot back under the table. Mum, seeing me lying there in the middle of the floor, screamed. She dropped down on her knees.

'Dave! Something's happened to Peony!'

Dennis thumped his back feet. Bang! Mum looked up. She screamed again. Then she noticed the hutch in the space under the stairs and the litter tray on the floor in front of the sink.

'What the...?'

'His name's Dennis,' I said, sitting up. 'He's a present from Gran.'

Dad appeared at the bottom of the stairs.

'How dare your mother dump this animal on us without so much as a by-your-leave? Or were you in on it?'

'Of course I wasn't!' goes Dad.

'Well you should have stopped her.'

'How?'

It was a fair question. Mum changed tack.

'Well, it can't stay. Put it out in the yard till we've worked out how to get rid of it.'

I said Dennis couldn't go outside. He was an indoor rabbit. He would catch a chill. He would be unhappy!

'But he's house-trained,' I added. 'He won't be any trouble.'

'No trouble!' Mum exploded. 'Who's going to feed him? Who's going to clean him out? Who's going to clear up his mess?'

Dad said he would be in charge of clearing up accidents – he showed Mum his stash of kitchen rolls. I said I would feed Dennis and clean out his hutch. Primrose, who had come to see what all the noise was about, said she would help with feeding and hutch-cleaning too, and do dry sweeps. 'But I'm not wiping up wee-wees,' she added. 'That's just disgusting!'

'Let's get this straight,' said Mum. 'The plan is for Dad to do cleaning up and you girls to co-operate together? It isn't going to work, is it?'

'Couldn't he have a sort of trial period?' asked Dad.

'Why?' said Mum. 'Oh, I see! You're scared of telling your mother we won't be keeping her mad present. You want to put off getting rid of him till after she's gone home.'

'Have you got a better idea?'

Mum made up her mind. 'All right,' she said. 'The rabbit's got one week. After that, if he's increasing the mess-and-stress levels in the house, he's got to go.'

She went to have a shower and get changed

out of her work clothes. Primrose, pouring a glass of water at the sink, spotted something weird in Dennis's litter tray. It looked like a small squishy slug. But on closer inspection, it was a poo.

I had read about this. Rabbits do two kinds of poos – small dry round ones and squishy ones they actually eat so they can get the goodness from their food twice over.

'He normally eats those ones,' I said.

'Yuk...gross!' goes Primrose.

Dad sloped off towards the stairs. Primrose checked her phone. She looked in the mirror. Then she went to do her nails. I looked at Dennis. It seemed to me he had about as much chance of passing his trial period as Primrose had of passing her exams.

Chapter 7
Gloomy Tunes and Teething Troubles

When I got downstairs the next morning Mum had already gone to work. Dad wouldn't be up any time soon and then he'd be off to watch a cricket match, and Primrose never got up until lunch-time on Sundays.

The door of Dennis's hutch was open. We hadn't shut it the night before because we thought he should be able to get to his litter tray if he wanted to go in the night. I looked in the bedroom end and he wasn't there. I looked under the table...no Dennis. I searched the whole kitchen but I couldn't find him.

I was beginning to panic when I noticed the back door was ajar and the washing was flapping on the line. Mum must have hung it out before she left and forgotten to shut the door. I went out into the yard.

Dennis was nibbling a plant in one of the big pots, stretching up on his back feet to reach. When he saw me he made a dash for the sun-lounger, diving for cover like a minnow in a rock-pool. Two enormous seagulls sitting on the wall screeched at each other as if to say, 'Where's our dinner gone?'

Our yard was sunk into the side of the hill with a wall round it. Mr Kaminski's garden, which was L-shaped, rose steeply beyond. Dennis wouldn't be able to get out but it still wasn't safe for him to be outside on his own.

Anything might happen. He might eat something poisonous – he might be attacked by gulls or cats. I stayed where I was, keeping still, and after what felt like five years he crept out from under the sun-lounger. He slowly sidled up and sniffed my bare toes.

I swooped down and scooped him up. I knew how to do that now from reading You and Your

Rabbit. You had to approach from above so the rabbit didn't see you coming. It seemed a bit of a mean trick but I wanted to get him inside.

The problem was, indoors was full of dangers too. In the book it said rabbits think wires are like roots, and when a rabbit is digging a burrow he bites through roots. There were wires all over the place in the kitchen. It was amazing Dennis had survived the night.

I almost wished Mum had made us take him back straight away instead of giving him a one-week trial. By the end of the week, I would be a nervous wreck!

The first thing Gran said when she arrived was, 'Why the long face?'

I explained about Mum leaving the back door open and Dennis being outside on his own and the kitchen being full of dangers too. Gran went straight into action. We had to build some barriers in case people forgot to shut the doors! We had to get some plastic tubing to cover all the wires!

'But it's not worth doing all that for just one week,' I protested.

'What do you mean, one week?'

I told her about Dennis's trial period. She smiled and put her arm round me.

'No-one would ever seriously want to get rid of a lovely rabbit like Dennis,' she said. She seemed to have forgotten that was exactly what his last owner did.

Gran told me to take Dad a cup of tea while she measured up how much tubing we would need to cover the wires. It would be too hard to do the whole house so she reckoned we should concentrate on the kitchen. It was a big room, plenty big enough for Dennis to run around in.

She said we would need low barricades across the bottom of the doors to keep Dennis in, in case anyone forgot to shut them. Knee-high should do because he was rather a fat rabbit and therefore not very bouncy. All us humans would easily be able to step over them.

Dad was not delighted to be woken up on a Sunday morning, and he was even less happy when I told him why. Gran was at the DIY store and she expected all hands on deck to help with the work as soon as she got back.

'All hands?' he said. 'Even Primrose? On a Sunday?'

No-one actually dared to wake Primrose up, and in the end she wandered down all on her own, droopy and bleary-eyed, when Dad started drilling and sawing.

'What's going on?'

I explained about the doors and the wires and the roots.

'Even a rabbit can't be so dim he'd mistake a wire for a root,' she said. 'That's just nuts.' Then she poured herself some cereal and sat down. She put her phone on the table beside her bowl, found some music and plugged her earphones in. You could see from her face that she was listening to gloomy tunes so it didn't take a genius to guess she still hadn't had a grovel-text from Matt.

We were so busy building barricades and covering wires that no-one noticed Dennis under the table looking at the loop of wire from Primrose's earphones, dangling over the edge. No-one saw him creep up to it. No-one saw him stretch up on his hind legs and snip clean through it with his teeth.

Primrose tapped her phone. She pressed some buttons. She took her earphones out, and saw the wire.

'He's bitten my earphones off!' she wailed. 'Now what am I supposed to do? I can't revise without music! I'm going to fail and it'll be his fault. Well...and Matt's,' she added.

There aren't any shops around here that sell stuff like earphones so Dad said he would order some new ones for her online.

'They'll be here tomorrow and in the meantime you can borrow Peony's.'

Charming! I mean, first she calls me nuts for saying Dennis might mistake a wire for a root, then she swipes my earphones when it turns out I was right!

We had just finished making the kitchen Dennis-proof when Mum came home for lunch. 'It's like Fort Knox in here,' she said, stepping over the barrier and closing the door after her. She noticed the plastic tubing on the wires. 'Is all this really necessary?'

Dad said yes it was, because it meant we could leave all the doors open and not have to worry about Dennis getting out. He opened the front door again to demonstrate.

Just then Mr Kaminski came up the steps, carrying a cake.

'I bring babka!' he goes. 'Is Polish cake... aaargh!' He banged into the barrier and pitched forwards into the kitchen. Dad made a grab for him.

Mr Kaminski somehow managed to hold onto the plate and not fall flat on his face but the cake flew up in the air. It spun like a Frisbee across the room and smacked into the far wall.

Mum checked that Mr Kaminski was all right; then she told Dad that his safety features were a hazard. They would have to go, but that didn't matter because so would Dennis.

'When I said he could have a week I was only thinking about mess-and-stress,' she said. 'It hadn't occurred to me that having a house rabbit might be dangerous.'

Mr Kaminski protested that it wasn't Dennis's fault. 'I am not careful,' he said. 'I am looking at babka.'

We all looked at the heap of lemony lumps and crumbs lying on the floor. Mum said she would like to invite Mr Kaminski to have supper with us the next day, by way of saying sorry. He was delighted. 'I bring new babka,' he said.

After he had gone Mum and Dad had a big row about who would actually be cooking this lovely supper. Monday was always Dad's busiest day for deadlines because the paper went to press on Tuesdays. 'Just because you work 24/7 that doesn't mean the rest of us aren't working too, you know!'

Luckily they couldn't go on too long because Mum had to get back to the Beach Hotel's hedges and Dad had to go to his cricket match. Primrose went to do a facial peel, which was supposed to make her look radiant. She still thought Matt would cave in and come over any minute. That's how well she knows him.

'It isn't working, is it?' I said to Gran. 'Having a pet really doesn't seem to be pulling us together.'

'You always get teething troubles,' said Gran, cheerfully. 'Give it time.'

'So, will you come over and make the supper tomorrow?' I asked. She shook her head. She had to go home in the morning because the surf school had a busy week coming up.

'But I'll visit again in a few weeks' time,' she said.

I love my Gran but sometimes I do wish she was less of an ideas person and just a little bit more boring.

Chapter 8
The Felt-tip Trick and the Bad, Bad Bunny

The next day at school I kept thinking about Dennis, all on his own at home. I wondered whether he was using his litter tray. I hoped he wasn't bored. The book said rabbits could get bored if they didn't have anything to play with, so I had tied a carrot on a piece of string and hung it from the underside of the table before I left. He would probably have eaten it all by now.

No-one else was in when I got home but

Primrose would be back soon. The first thing I noticed was that there weren't any pees and poos on the floor – they were all in the litter tray. Well done, Dennis! I moved it a few inches further over towards the space under the stairs.

Then I spotted Dennis sitting on top of his hutch, half hidden by the bumper pack of kitchen rolls. I couldn't get at him from above so it was no good trying to pick him up. He'd just go mental and shoot off round the room like a rocket.

I peeped under the table to see how he had been getting on with his carrot. It was completely un-nibbled. The nearest table leg, on the other hand, was covered in tooth marks. Dennis had gnawed great chunks out of the varnish leaving scratches and patches of pale bare wood.

I sat down on the floor to get a closer look at the damage. Dennis hopped down off his hutch roof and came over. He was very sweet to look at but considering he was single-handedly wrecking our kitchen, Gran might have done more for family harmony if she'd given us a herd of galloping rhinos.

Primrose arrived home and Dennis shot back up into his hidey-hole behind the kitchen-rolls. She dropped her bag on the floor with a big sigh. Then she took her earphones out – well, *my* earphones, actually, which Dad had only said she could use for doing her revision, not to take to school.

'What is the matter with him?' she grumbled, as she poured herself a glass of water.

'I don't know,' I said. 'It doesn't say anything in the book about eating furniture.'

'Not him, Peony,' she snapped. 'Matt! How could he mess me about like this?'

'So he hasn't texted yet, then?'

'What do *you* think?'

I thought it was a bit much her taking it out on me when she was the one who got herself into this mess.

'Maybe when you said he needn't bother coming round any more, he thought you actually meant it,' I suggested.

'Well, I might have meant it at the time, but I obviously didn't mean it forever.'

'You'd better text him then, because that will no way be obvious to Matt. Why don't you ask him round tonight?'

She sat down beside me on the floor with her phone in her hand.

'Woah!' she said, suddenly noticing the table leg. 'Mum's going to freak.' Then, because she's got the attention-span of an earwig, she straightaway asked, 'Do you really think I should text him?'

I nodded and, to my surprise, she started texting.

'You could fix that with a brown felt-tip,' she added, not looking up.

Big sisters are ninety-nine per cent nuisance but one per cent good advice because they've been around longer and know more tricks and dodges. I dug around in the table drawer, found a dark brown felt-tip pen and started colouring in the pale patches.

The felt-tip trick worked a treat. You could hardly see where Dennis had chewed the varnish off. Primrose paced up and down all the time I was doing it, fretting about whether she should have sent that text.

'Let's make some toast,' I said, 'while we're waiting for him to reply.'

It was a tense wait, considering that if texting didn't work it would be my fault for suggesting it.

'Send him a picture of Dennis too,' I said, thinking I might as well get it in the neck for two failed texts as for one.

She sent the picture while I put the marge and peanut butter on the table and found some knives and plates. We were spreading our toast when Primrose got the text-tone. She jumped, dropping the marge lid on the floor in her hurry to read it.

She stared at her message in disbelief. 'He isn't coming,' she said. She showed me his text:

```
you finished with me, can't come
anyway, exam tmo, Matt
```

'He didn't even put love, or a smiley, or let's talk. He didn't even say about Dennis,' she said.

It did seem surprisingly cold for Matt, who is usually lovely.

'What exactly did you say to him?'

She scrolled through her messages and read her text.

```
I have decided to forgive you.
You can come round tonight
```

Way to make someone feel like coming back to you!

Just then she got a second text – it said,

```
what's with the rabbit?
```

She texted back that Dennis was living in our kitchen but he'd be gone by next week, sad but true.

We waited but Matt didn't text again.

'This was a stupid idea,' Primrose said. 'Now I feel like an idiot. I should never have listened to you!'

'I said you should text him. I didn't say you

should send him a sniffy message from the top of your high horse and make him run a mile.'

'Whatever,' goes Primrose. 'Anyway, he needn't think I'm going to forgive him again!'

There was a funny squishy noise coming from under the table. We both bent down to look. It was Dennis licking a big lump of marge off the lid Primrose had dropped. She reached out to grab it off him...and he bit her!

Primrose screamed. She pulled away, bumping her head under the table. Dennis thumped his back feet on the floor.

'You're frightening him,' I said.

She shoved her hand under my nose.

'He bit me!' she yelled. 'Look at that – blood!'

Dennis grabbed the lid in his teeth and made off across the kitchen with it. He dragged it to safety under his hutch.

'Yes, but could you be a bit quieter? Rabbits don't like noise.'

'I don't care about that!' shouted Primrose. 'I don't even like him! He's turning out to be a complete pain. He bit through my earphones yesterday and now he's bitten me. Wait till I tell Mum!'

She stormed out of the kitchen and stamped off up the stairs. I got the barbecue tongs out of the drawer and tried to get the marge lid off

Dennis, but he wasn't having any of it. Rabbits must really like the taste of marge.

Mum came home with a quiche from the baker's, and then Dad brought a bag of salad – they must have done a deal on who was making supper. Mr Kaminski arrived as we were setting the table. He stepped very carefully over the barrier and delivered his newly-baked lemon babka safely into my hands. He was wearing a smart shirt and his white hair was combed back.

'Your grandmother is here soon, yes?'

When I said she wasn't coming he looked like the boy Father Christmas forgot.

Mum said, 'Supper's ready. Where's Primrose?'

At that very moment, Primrose came down the stairs holding her arm as if her hand might fall off if she let go. She had about fifty plasters stuck over the bite.

'I need a rabies injection!' she announced.

Then she launched into a great long moan about how Dennis had bitten her when she wasn't even doing anything, unless trying to stop him from munching his way through a plastic lid and probably getting poisoned counted as provocation. What if she got an infection in the wound, and her hand swelled up to five times its normal size? She would get carted off to hospital and they would pump her full of drugs. But what if the drugs didn't work and they ended up chopping her hand off? It could happen!

While Mum was peeling away the plasters Mr Kaminski tried to get Dad to talk about the problem page. He felt really bad about never answering any of the letters about family stuff and he had brought the one from Frantic Mum to talk about again. It had been most helpful, he said, talking about it before, but for some reason he didn't seem to feel any more confident about answering it.

One of Dad's favourite sayings is 'never do today what you can put off until tomorrow'.

'Let's discuss it over coffee in the morning,' he said.

Mr K didn't look very happy about it but before he could say anything Dennis hopped down off his hutch roof, giving Dad a perfect opportunity to change the subject.

'I'm surprised you're willing to show your face, young Dennis,' he said. 'Because it sounds like you have been a bad, bad bunny!'

Chapter 9
Choc Sauce and the
Last Chance Saloon

Here's a top tip you won't find in You and Your Rabbit – never let your rabbit go anywhere near margarine. After Mr Kaminski had gone home Dad went to the pub, Mum got Stella round to do some paperwork in the sitting-room upstairs... and Dennis started producing a third kind of poo.

I won't go into details in case you're eating your tea but he was like a walking squeezy bottle of chocolate sauce. It squirted out of him so fast, in five minutes the whole floor was covered in smelly spits and splats. I grabbed some kitchen roll and started trying to clean it up quick, but he just kept doing more and more.

Primrose was outside in the yard, sighing into her socks, but she never lasts long without an audience so she soon came in looking for someone to grumble at. She stood in the doorway gawping at all the little heaps of scrunched-up dirty kitchen roll and puddles of poo.

'He's got the runs from eating that marge,' I said. 'You're the one who dropped the lid so you should help me clean it up.'

'Not happening!' said Primrose. 'Wouldn't be happening even if I didn't have an open wound from where he blooming bit me.'

'Well, at least you could check he's OK. He's gone under his hutch and I'm worried about him.'

'Read my lips, Peony,' she goes. 'I do not care whether he's OK. I do not like him. I am officially Not Interested in that vicious little brute!'

'But...'

She stuffed my earphones into her ears and picked her way through the clumps of kitchen roll to the stairs.

'And use some disinfectant,' she said, as she left, 'or we'll all end up catching it.'

I didn't think humans could catch rabbit-runs but just to be on the safe side I got the disinfectant out from under the sink. I poured some into a bucket and topped it up with hot water like they do at school if someone's been sick. Then I bunged all the bits of dirty kitchen roll in the bin and got the mop.

Mopping is actually a lot more difficult than you might think. In no time at all, the floor was soaking wet and the more I mopped, the wetter it seemed to get. I went and put my wellies on.

I topped up the bucket because it was nearly empty, and when I turned round again there was Dennis standing by my feet looking up at me. On the upside, he hadn't died from diarrhoea – on the downside, he was knee-deep in disinfectant. Supposing it was bad for him, like marge? He would lick it off cleaning himself and then... I scooped him up and stood him in the empty sink.

I ran the tap lukewarm and washed Dennis's feet. He was a bit droopy and didn't struggle at all. Then I lifted him onto a tea-towel and dried him off. I was going to put him in his hutch while I finished mopping the floor but he looked so sorry for himself that I wondered if he might let me hold him.

I sat down on a chair with Dennis in my lap.

He didn't jump off. The fur on his back was thick and soft; his ears were velvety and very warm. It says in You and Your Rabbit that rabbits don't sweat, so if they get hot they let the heat out through their ears. I hoped he didn't have a temperature.

Anyway, there I was in my wellies, with Dennis on my lap and the kitchen looking like one of those news stories about people whose houses have got flooded, when Mum and Stella walked in.

'Maybe I'll skip that coffee, Jan,' goes Stella. She shot through on tip-toes, stepped over the barrier and was out the front door faster than John Foster, the fastest boy in school.

Mum pressed her lips together and took a deep breath.

'It's not his fault,' I mumbled. 'H-he ate some marge and got the runs and I was trying to clean it up but then...'

'Put him in his hutch,' said Mum.

She picked up the mop and by some miracle, instead of making the floor get wetter and wetter, her mopping seemed to dry the water up.

'Clean that sink out! Put that tea-towel in the washing-machine! Take those wellington boots off and stop making filthy footprints on the floor!' She barked orders at me while she mopped.

When she had finished she shoved the mop and bucket out in the yard, slammed the door shut and told me she had enough on her plate without all this nonsense. It was one thing after another and how could she ever get her business up and running when she was always having to clean up after us lot?

'And don't cry!'

'I'm not crying,' I blubbed.

Mum calmed down as quickly as she had flared up. She gave me a hug. 'I'm sorry, Peony,' she sighed. 'I'm not cross with you. I'm cross with your father. And Gran – she really doesn't help. Buying us a house rabbit – I mean, what was she thinking?'

I couldn't tell Mum what Gran was thinking because it just seemed nutty now. But sometimes although Gran's great ideas don't work the way she thinks they're going to, something good can come out of them.

The bed-and-breakfast, for example – that was a disaster but it did mean they got pots more money when they sold their house than they would have done before they converted it into a B&B, and then they could afford a really nice house in Spain with a pool and everything. Not that that ended up the way Gran thought it would either, but still.

Dennis wasn't going to make my family any less of a pain and he wasn't even much of a pet, not like a dog you could train or a cat you could cuddle up with. He wasn't like lovely old Sam.

But Dennis was better than nothing. I had never had a pet and I was pretty sure I never would have if Gran hadn't gone out and got Dennis without asking Mum and Dad.

I knew I would end up doing all the work, feeding him and cleaning his hutch, covering up for him when he wrecked things. But whatever happened, I was determined to try and hang onto him.

'Peony,' Mum said in a you-aren't-going-to-like-this kind of voice. 'You do realise that Dennis has to go now, don't you? This is the third time he's been a danger to life and limb, what with Mr Kaminski nearly breaking his neck falling over the barrier and Primrose getting that nasty bite and now the whole of the kitchen – the kitchen, mind, the place we prepare food and eat – being covered in germy deposits.'

'But he's in his trial period,' I protested. 'He's got another four days.'

I was still feeling a bit wobbly from before and it seemed a good moment not to try and hold back the tears.

Mum sighed. 'All right, he can have one more

chance,' she said. 'One more, Peony – I mean it. That rabbit really is drinking in the Last Chance Saloon.'

Chapter 10
'You're the Boss!' and Birthday Plans

I was sitting at the computer in the kitchen talking to Gran on Skype. Dennis hopped over and nudged my foot. I lifted my toes and he flattened himself to the floor, pushing his head underneath them. When rabbits do that they're saying, 'You're the boss!' I read about it in my book.

It was Friday evening and ever since the marge mishap Dennis had been different. He was more friendly towards me and less friendly towards Primrose. It was her own fault, really. After he had bitten her she had made this big thing of being scared of him to get the sympathy vote. He could be minding his own business or having one of his mad random dashes round the room and she would suddenly screech and jump up on a chair.

'Come off it, Primrose, he was nowhere near you,' I would say. But Mum fell for it every time. 'He has bitten her, Peony. It's not surprising she feels nervous around him.'

The problem was, after a few days Dennis seemed to make up his mind that if she didn't like him then he didn't like her either. Then he really did start growling and running at her ankles whenever she came near. He tried to nip her, and although it doesn't say so in the book I'm pretty sure that means 'Watch out – I'm the boss of you!'

'How's your week been?' Gran asked. The picture was a bit slower than the sound, but it was brilliant to see her face. We used to Skype all the time before the summer visitors arrived and the surf school got so busy.

I told her we had managed to move Dennis's litter tray bit by bit all the way into the space under the stairs now. I mentioned the table leg, and the fact that no-one seemed to have noticed. Then I gave her the full story of what happened when Dennis ate the marge.

'But he hasn't had any more mishaps since then,' I said.

'It sounds as if he's passed his trial period with flying colours!' goes Gran.

Then I told her about Primrose. 'She hates him,' I said. 'She's really got it in for him. She's been pointing her fingers at him like a gun and saying, "One more day, buddy – one more day!" It's not fair because she winds him up. Otherwise I know he wouldn't keep going for her.'

Primrose was definitely not going to let Mum forget that tomorrow was the end of Dennis's trial period. The only thing that could possibly distract her was if Matt should miraculously walk through the door and fall at her feet in a grateful heap because she had forgiven him. Which was about as likely as a chunk of France floating across the channel and attaching itself to Polgotherick.

For once in her life, Gran was flummoxed.

'It'd be such a shame if Dennis had to go because he hasn't had time to get used to Primrose yet. If we could just get him a few more weeks I'm sure he would settle down,' she said. 'Still, nothing can happen before you get home from the kennels tomorrow, so we've got until lunch-time to think of something.'

Gran says often her best ideas kind of creep up on her when she isn't looking, so she changed the subject and we got talking about all sorts of other things, such as her old bones.

'My old bones can't seem to take this surfing malarkey any more,' she said. 'After two hours in the surf, I need another two on the settee to recover. I'm thinking I might have to hang up my wetsuit at the end of this season.'

'If you weren't working at the surf school we could see you more often,' I said. 'You could come up here on my birthday like you used to when I was little.'

'Your birthday!' said Gran. 'That's the solution!'

Gran said Mum and Dad could no way get rid of Dennis in the run-up to my birthday because they wouldn't want to spoil the day. Therefore I should start talking about my birthday straight away, so they couldn't ignore the fact it was only next week.

'And don't settle for a tea-party or something after school on the day,' Gran said. 'Ask for a weekend treat, like the time they took you to Alton Towers or that camping trip to Smugglers' Cove. Then Dennis will be with you for another whole week and another weekend after that, and by that time this trial period thing will be a distant memory.'

I wasn't sure about it. Dennis would be a nightmare in a tent. He'd chew through all the guy-lines and try to burrow out. But Gran said we wouldn't have to take him with us. He'd be perfectly happy at home. He wasn't like a dog or cat that would pine and need feeding every day.

'In that way, a rabbit is an ideal pet,' she said. 'Remember to mention that fact!'

So the next day after my shift at the kennels I got stuck in talking about my birthday before Mum had even got the fish and chips out of their wrappings. Mum said she could stop work early on my birthday and we could all go to the open day at Gulhaven Gardens. The wisteria there was world-class, she assured us.

'Peony doesn't want to visit some boring old garden on her birthday!' Dad said. 'Besides, England's playing that night. She'd much rather go to the pub and watch the match on the big screen with a nice bag of crisps and a glass of lemonade.'

Primrose said they were outrageously only thinking about themselves. I was a girl and therefore I would obviously want a proper girlie birthday a trip to Beachside Beauty for example. 'They do hair and nails for forty quid,' she said.

'I bet we could get a deal for the whole family.'

Mum pointed out that nice hair wasn't that important when you spent your days hacking through brambles.

'And fancy nails aren't really the thing for a sports reporter,' said Dad.

Primrose took the huff. 'So what are we going to do?' she said. 'Because I'm not walking round some smelly old wisteria or sitting in the pub with Dad. That's just embarrassing!'

'Actually, I was thinking I'd really like a weekend trip this year,' I said.

No-one seemed very keen but I ploughed on.

'I'd like to go camping at Smugglers' Cove again. That was my best birthday ever!'

Mum said maybe camping wasn't the best thing to do this year because normally she organised everything and she didn't have time to do stuff like that right now. It would be up to Dad, and we all knew he had the organisational skills of a potato.

Dad bristled. How hard could it be to throw a few things in the back of the car? He could do it just as well as Mum and he wouldn't mind having a chance to prove it! It was actually a good time for him too, because they had a student on work experience at the paper who could cover the weekend matches.

'What about Dennis?' goes Primrose. 'He can't come camping. Oh, but of course he'll be gone by next weekend. I mean, he's had his trial period and – '

'Dennis can stay at home,' I interrupted. 'He doesn't need lots of attention like a cat or dog. He's a perfect pet in that way, when you come to think about it.'

'We'll worry about Dennis later,' said Mum. 'I think Peony's birthday plans are more important right now.'

Nice try, Primrose, but it looked like game, set and match to Peony. Well, with a little bit of help from Gran!

Chapter 11
A Crushed Cake and a Little Bit of Breeze

Dennis was as good as gold all week. He did scatter a few poos in unlikely places but I swept them up quick-smart before anyone else noticed.

I couldn't wait to get home from school every day and see him. As soon as I sat down on the floor he would come over and give me a good sniff. Sometimes he would let me stroke him without running away. I would share my snack with him, a bit of banana or raw carrot, or a corner of toast – without any marge on it, obviously.

You couldn't really cuddle Dennis but you could talk to him. He didn't suddenly leave you hanging in the middle of a sentence because he had more important things to do like Mum, or go nuts over nothing like Primrose, or have one ear on the radio like Dad.

I wasn't the only one who liked talking to Dennis either. Dad was always doing it – 'I'm going to read the paper now, Dennis. Do you want to come out in the yard for a bit?' Mum said hello to him whenever she passed through the kitchen, and Primrose muttered at him: 'You need anger management, you do,' and 'Your days are numbered, buddy.'

Dennis still didn't like Primrose and he often went for her, but that wasn't surprising because she was in such a grumpy mood all the time. I wouldn't have minded going for her myself. She stamped and crashed and flopped around.

It was bad enough, Primrose said, that Matt had knocked back her invitation when she had so graciously forgiven him, and for such a flimsy excuse as having an exam the next day. But that exam was a whole week ago now and he still hadn't been back in touch.

'He's putting me in a difficult position,' she grumbled. 'That's twice he's been horrible – I can't forgive him again!'

She didn't even stop banging on about it on my actual birthday, which was the Thursday. It wasn't as if I was expecting a full-on birthday tea, what with having a trip at the weekend and everything, but I did think she might take a few hours off to think about someone else on their birthday.

'I mean, what if he just turns up at the door?' goes Primrose, checking herself in the mirror. Then, checking her phone, 'What if he texts me and wants to come round?'

I seriously snapped.

'He isn't going to come, and he isn't going to text. I know him.'

It was true. I knew Matt better than she did, from working at the kennels. But she didn't want to listen.

'You're wrong – he really likes me!'

'He really liked you, past tense. Then you had your hissy fit and you haven't got down off your high horse ever since. It is possible to go off people, you know.'

I told Primrose that if she wanted Matt back she had to stop worrying about whether to forgive him and ask him to forgive her.

'You've been really moody to him. You're the one who should say sorry.'

She took that about as well as those tone-deaf people on The X Factor do when Simon Cowell tells them they can't sing. But on the upside, it did seem to shut her up, and the good effects lasted right through Friday. She still flounced around looking tragic, but at least she wasn't bending our ears all the time.

On Saturday morning Dad had to get up early to take me to the kennels because Becky was still on holiday and Mum was working until lunchtime. The weather was sunny, perfect for camping, and Dad was quite fired up about it.

He had the whole morning to get everything packed and sorted and as he said, he could virtually do that with his eyes shut, we had been camping in France so many times. He didn't need Mum around to issue orders!

By the time he came back to pick me up everything was apparently sorted. He told me he had bought the food and packed the camping stuff into the car. It had indeed been easy peasy lemon squeezy, just as he had expected.

'Your mother will have to take back that rude thing she said about my organisational skills,' he told me as we walked down the path from the car.

'Oh, there you are Dave,' said Mum the minute we walked in the door. 'Where's the bread?'

'Already packed,' said Dad.

'And the milk?'

'That's packed as well.'

'So what are we having for lunch?' goes Mum.

The plan had been to have some sandwiches before we left, but Dad must have forgotten.

'I...thought we could wait till we get there?' tried Dad.

Mum rolled her eyes and sighed. Primrose crossed her arms over her chest and tapped her foot impatiently. I topped up Dennis's food and water while they argued it out. It wasn't a perfect start to the weekend but it did mean things could only get better.

Smugglers' Cove is an hour down the coast but it seems much longer when you're starving hungry. Dad had the radio turned up to stop Mum going on at him and Primrose was fiddling about with her phone. I was playing that game where you try to make a headline from the number-plate letters of passing cars. FDC... Family Deafened in Car! ETP...Elephant Tramples Phone!

'OK, I've done it,' Primrose said. 'I've said sorry. Since you seem to think that's what he wants.'

It would have been better if she'd said sorry because she meant it, but whatever.

'When?'

'Just now,' she said. 'I've just pressed send.' Then, seeing my face, 'What?'

I shrugged.

She would remember soon enough that there's no mobile reception at Smugglers' Cove. Matt couldn't text her back now even if he wanted to.

The campsite was nearly full. It's only small, not much more than a toilet block in a field, but we like it because it's only one minute's walk from the beach. The first time I ever went there was with Toby and his family – they know all the little out-of-the-way campsites.

My other best friend from school, Jess, once looked up why it was called Smugglers' Cove. She found out it wasn't proper olden days smugglers with rum and cutlasses and everything, but some people smuggling drugs in on boats thirty years ago. Right up till then it had been called St Keverne's Cove. Then she looked up St Keverne. She looks everything up.

When we started to pitch the tent we realised Dad had forgotten to pack the mallet. On the upside he had also forgotten the pegs so there wasn't anything to hammer in.

'Not to worry,' he said, cheerfully. 'We can always borrow some!'

With that, he went round the whole site asking people if they could spare us a few pegs. So embarrassing! In the meantime, Mum unpacked the food box and discovered we had hardly anything to eat except baked beans, bread and a bought birthday cake.

'We might as well eat all this for lunch,' she said. 'Someone will have to go and find a food shop later anyway.'

Mum lit the stove and cooked the beans while Dad bashed the handful of pegs he'd managed to scrounge into the ground with a stone. We scoffed the beans and then moved on to the cake. It was in a white box from the baker's shop on Ship Lane. Dad had got them to write 'Happy Birthday' on it in red icing, which was nice, but he hadn't remembered to get any candles.

It didn't seem likely we'd be able to scrounge any birthday-cake candles so Mum suggested we stick one of our emergency supply of normal candles in the cake and light that instead.

The cake looked a lot less pretty with a household candle stuck in the middle of it. It seemed somehow crushed and disappointed with itself. To make things worse, the candle kept blowing out before they finished singing.

Mum said the fact that the wind was getting up might be bad news for anyone whose tent only had five pegs holding it down.

'It's just a little bit of breeze,' goes Dad. 'It's nothing to worry about!'

Chapter 12
The Dead of the Night and Dennis's Disappearing Whiskers

I was dreaming we were all in a boat far out on the open sea. The waves were huge and the boat was pitching up, up, up to the top of each one and then down, down, down into the trough between them. It was like a roller-coaster ride, except it wasn't fun. My heart was beating so hard I couldn't breathe.

I saw this super-massive wave coming towards us. The closer it got, the bigger it looked. It towered over us like a black mountain of water. The boat climbed up, up, up until it was perched on the very top of the enormous wave.

I looked down at my hands, gripping onto the rail. My knuckles were as white as bone. The wind was whipping up the spray. Everything was soaking wet, my hair, my clothes. I could feel the water streaming down my face and taste the salt on my lips. The boat tipped and started to plunge. I opened my mouth to cry out.

'Wake up, Peony!' Mum was shaking my shoulder. 'Wake up!'

The nightmare faded away but then I seemed to wake up in another one. It was pitch dark and there was a storm-force gale howling round the tent, pushing right up under the groundsheet, prising it up from the ground like a giant peeling off a sticker.

'We're all going to die!' cried Primrose. Mum stopped shaking me and shone the torch towards her.

'We're not going to die, Primrose. We're going to keep calm, that's what we're going to do.'

The living-room end suddenly lifted clean off the ground. The cooker toppled over and a pile of plastic cups and plates came cascading into the bedroom area. The groundsheet settled back for a few seconds but then another gust got underneath and the box with all the food in it fell over.

'Where's Dad?' I yelled above the howling of the wind.

'Outside attaching the guy-lines.'

'What's he attaching them to? We haven't got any pegs!'

'The roof rack on the car, next door's tow-hook, the post with the pitch number on... I don't know, Peony. Just anything he can find.'

Mum said while Dad was fixing the guy-lines we three should pack everything up ready to empty the tent out.

'When he thinks it will hold, we'll shift everything into the car,' she said.

'But what if—?' Primrose began.

'Before we get into "what ifs", have you got a better plan?'

Primrose was shivering so hard she could barely shake her head.

'Well, then,' said Mum.

We pulled our coats on over our pj's and started stuffing things into bags and boxes. The wind, pushing under the groundsheet, brought it up in big bubbles around our feet. It tugged at the roof, sucking it this way and that. It flung things across the tent and drowned our voices with its rushing noise.

Dad came round to the front and opened the zip a few inches. The door was on the lee-side so nothing terrible happened and he opened it right up.

'It should be OK now,' he said. 'But let's be quick!'

We'd only got half the stuff out when the tent suddenly lifted and several guy-lines pinged off.

'It's getting away!' yelled Dad. 'Primrose, Peony – grab a corner!'

The three of us clung on to the tent while Mum got the last few things out, then we released the poles and collapsed it down. As soon as it was flat on the ground it stopped flapping and gave up trying to get away.

We rolled the tent up and bundled it into the car. Then we piled in after it. Dad switched the engine on so we could get the heater going. He didn't drive off straight away but waited, as if there was another choice except giving up and going home.

We sat there in the dark car, no-one saying anything. Dad drove slowly down the bumpy track and out onto the lane. It may be only an hour up the road from Smugglers' Cove to home but it feels a lot longer in the dead of the night, when you're freezing cold and fed up.

At times like these the last thing you want is to have to leave your car at the top of the hill and walk down the steep zig-zag path to your house. The second-to-last thing you want is to get to your house and find your next-door neighbour, Mr Kaminski, outside in his dressing-gown peering in the front window.

'You home!' he cried. 'Thank goodness heavens!'

'Whatever is the matter, Mr Kaminski?' goes Mum.

'Are you all right?' goes Dad.

'I all right yes, but I hear big bang. I don't know what is. I try to see inside.'

Mum said she was sure everything was fine, and perhaps he had been dreaming? Dad unlocked the front door and flicked the light switch. Nothing happened. He felt his way across to the light above the sink and tried that one. Again, nothing.

'We seem to have blown a fuse,' he said. He found the emergency torch and switched that on.

'Something else seems different,' said Mum.

We huddled in the doorway, spooked by the darkness, while Dad fiddled about in the fuse box.

'The fridge light!' Mum exclaimed. 'It's off and it should always be on.'

Dad fixed the fuse and the lights came on, but the little red light on the fridge was still off.

'It's probably the fuse in the plug then,' he said, pulling the fridge out from under the work-top to have a look. He stopped pulling and gave a low whistle.

'This is not good...'

Dad unplugged the fridge. He brought the plug out from under the work surface and a length of wire came after it. The wire looked as if it had been sliced open. You could see the metal strands inside. Dennis!

The gap between the cupboards and the fridge was so narrow we thought he'd never be able to squeeze through, so we hadn't bothered to cover the wires at the back.

Dennis wasn't in his hutch, or underneath it, or on the roof, which were his three favourite places in the night. We found him under the table. His eyes were wide and his nose was twitching even more than usual. I dropped on my knees and reached under, not worrying he might try to bite me. I got my hands round his behind and slid him across the floor towards me.

All the whiskers had gone from one side of his face, snipped short and frizzled at the ends.

'Is incredible,' Mr Kaminski gasped. 'He bites wire, he should be dead.'

Mr Kaminski was looking half-dead himself, with his hair sticking out and his skin kind of grey. Mum did what she always does at such times – she made everyone a cup of tea.

As we sat round the table, gradually warming up and calming down, Dad told Mr Kaminski all about our camping catastrophe.

'It's been a birthday trip when everything went wrong,' Mum said. 'But I bet we'll look back on it in years to come and think it was quite funny.'

'I won't,' I thought to myself. 'I'll look back on it as the birthday when Mum was too busy to make me a cake, Dad was too lazy to organise my trip properly, and Primrose spent the whole time trying to find a patch of signal for her phone. I'll remember it as the time yet another of Gran's great ideas went pear-shaped; the time when Dennis lost half his wonderful whiskers and nearly got himself killed.'

Chapter 13
A Magnificent Mansion and the Family Facts of Life

'Peony!'

Miss Thomson stopped me as I was about to leave. It had been the longest school-day since the dinosaurs roamed the earth so I wasn't that delighted.

'Yes, Miss Thomson?'

'Is something wrong? Only I've noticed you don't seem quite your normal self today.'

'No, I'm fine...thank you.'

She gave me that X-ray look you sometimes get from teachers which makes you feel like they can see right through you. I looked down at my shoes, and finally she nodded and let me go.

My chat with Miss Thomson meant I was a bit late getting home. As I turned the last bend on the zig-zag path before our house I heard a weird noise that sounded like an animal in pain. I stopped for a few seconds to listen. My heart sank. I knew that noise – it was Primrose!

Primrose's bedroom was at the front of the house. She had her window wide open and the sound of her wailing was wafting out.

'Ohhh...ohhh...o-o-ohhh...'

She must have heard from Matt at last, but not the news she wanted to hear. It was so embarrassing. How could she make such an exhibition of herself? All the neighbours would hear. So would the tourists strolling past and the boy putting leaflets through letterboxes. They could probably hear her down at the beach and up on the top road. She could at least shut her window.

The sound of Primrose wailing didn't do anything to help me with my own bad mood. It wasn't just about my birthday trip. Lots of special days go wrong, like Primrose's 13th birthday party at the ice rink when three people ended up in casualty, or that Christmas when we all went down with food poisoning. You can get over that kind of thing, it's just life.

The problem was Dennis. It was one thing to poo all over the place or bite someone's hand or need barriers that tripped the neighbours up, but it was quite another thing to nearly set fire to the house while everyone was away for the weekend, and that's what could have happened when he bit through the wire, according to Mum, Dad and Mr Kaminski.

Dennis wasn't just a bit of a health hazard – he was a disaster waiting to happen, and even I could see now that he would have to go.

Dad was sitting in the sunshine doing some work on his laptop when I got home. There was a heap of empty boxes stacked up in the corner of the yard that Mum's new gardening equipment had come in. Having nothing but a patch of concrete out the back meant we had never had any need for things like lawnmowers, hedge-cutters or strimmers before.

'Dennis is out here if you're looking for him,' Dad said. 'He seems quite keen on cardboard!'

Dennis was sitting in one of the boxes, washing his face. He always looked his most adorable when he was washing. I sat down nearby and he came out to say hello, lying just near enough for me to stroke him but too far away for me to pick him up.

'Do you think Mum still wants those boxes?' I asked Dad.

He shook his head. 'I shouldn't think so.'

'Can I have one then?'

In the book it said you could make a house for your rabbit out of a cardboard box. You just had to close the top and cut some doors and windows for him to hop in and out. I wanted to make Dennis's last few days with us especially nice for him.

I chose the lawnmower box because it was big and sturdy. I stuck the top down with Sellotape and tried to cut a door, but the scissors wouldn't go through.

'Want some help?' asked Dad. He got a sharp knife and asked me where I wanted him to cut.

We cut a door big enough for Dennis to squeeze through. Then we moved right away from it. Sure enough after a few minutes he got curious and went to investigate. He pushed at the flap with his nose. He scratched at the sides of the door with his front paws. He nibbled bits off it. When he had adjusted the door to his satisfaction he wriggled inside.

Dennis was delighted with his little house. We

could hear him scrabbling and scratching around in there. I went to get some hay to make it cosy.

'You know what?' said Dad. 'Why don't we make him an upstairs?'

I coaxed Dennis back out with a bit of biscuit so Dad could cut a hole in the roof. Then he got another box and cut a hole in the bottom of that and put it on top. He stuck it down with lots of Sellotape. He cut a little window too so Dennis could look out.

As soon as we let him go back inside, Dennis hopped into his upstairs and peeped out of the window. Dad looked at me. Yes – we should make a third floor! He got another box.

Dad decided to take Dennis's house indoors before it got too big to move. I followed with all the other boxes. One of them was long and thin so we made a tunnel for Dennis from his house to his favourite sunny spot in the corner by the radiator. One was small and square so we stuck it on the side as a spare bedroom.

Pretty soon we had used all the boxes and we stood back to admire our handiwork. We hadn't just made a house – we had made a magnificent mansion! We could hear Dennis thumping and jumping and scratching away happily inside.

The phone went and Dad picked it up. I could tell from his side of the conversation that it was

Mum and she wasn't going to be home for tea. Some woman from Polgotherick Properties had asked her to look at a garden on her way home.

'You know Nash House?' Dad said, as he put the phone down. Of course I knew Nash House. Everyone knew it. It stood at the end of a grassy path that ran towards the headland from the top end of our terrace. No-one had lived there for years.

The garden was like a jungle and the house was falling apart because when the old man who owned it died, they couldn't find the nephew he had left it to. Well it turned out the nephew was living in America and now they'd finally found him he wasn't interested in the house at all.

'He wants to sell it,' Dad said. 'He's getting it done up first because he doesn't think anyone's going to want it in the state it's in.'

'So are they going to ask Mum to do the garden?'

Dad nodded. He said Mum was over the moon because she'd always wanted to have a proper nosey around up there. A high stone wall ran right round the property and the gate was boarded over and padlocked, so you couldn't even get a glimpse of the garden through the bars.

'I can see why she's keen,' he sighed. 'But I wish she would rein it in a bit. I mean, she can't ever do anything by halves, your mother. Look what she was like when she worked at the Green Fingers Garden Centre. We couldn't move in here for rescued plants!'

'Gran says that's just the way she is,' I said. 'She's like a busy bee that loves to buzz around.'

'What, you've talked to Gran about this?'

'Yes. I don't like Mum being out all the time either. But Gran says you can't change someone's nature – you just have to live with it.'

'I see,' goes Dad.

'You can't change a lazy old lion either,' I said. He knew who I was talking about all right!

I told him gloomily that Gran said you could choose your friends but you couldn't choose your family. You had to get on with them whatever they were like. Those were the family facts of life.

I didn't bother to mention she'd also said you could learn to like them, because I didn't believe it.

Dad said, 'Look, Peony, I've been meaning to tell you, I'm really sorry about your birthday trip. I should have organised it better.'

Then he got all embarrassed and started searching through the cupboards to see what we could have for tea.

'Tell you what,' he said. 'Why don't we do a supermarket order online – you could help me decide what we need. Let's fill up the cupboards and try some new recipes!'

'Seriously?' I said.

'I'm bored with beans,' goes Dad. 'I'm thinking – how hard can it be to cook a curry?'

Chapter 14
The Wailing Stage and the Wonder of Dennis

The supermarket couldn't deliver the food we ordered until the next day but now that Dad had had the idea, he was determined to try and cook a curry. He had another dig around in the cupboards and came out with a tin of tomatoes, a jar of curry powder and some chick peas. Then he found a few sad carrots, a soft potato and some sprouting onions in the bottom of the fridge.

Following the recipe on the side of the curry powder he somehow managed to produce a not-bad curry. All right, you had to mix it with a lot of rice or else it would blow the top of your head off, and all right, the rice was thick and sticky like mashed potato – but I didn't care. It wasn't beans, and it gave Primrose something else to think about apart from Matt.

She disappeared back upstairs after supper and Dad put the leftover curry and rice on a plate for Mum to warm up in the microwave later. He was dead chuffed with himself. She was going to be so impressed!

Unfortunately, the first thing she saw when she came in was Dennis's mansion. Well, you couldn't really miss it. Dad and I were putting a tall chimney made out of toilet rolls on the top. Dennis didn't need it but it definitely added to the look.

'I don't believe this,' said Mum. 'Honestly, Dave! You've got time for messing around with boxes but you can't be bothered to cook a proper tea for your children!'

Dad said he had cooked a proper tea tonight, as a matter of fact, and she would find hers in the microwave all ready for heating up. Plus, he had ordered a whole lot of food – actual vegetables and stuff – from the supermarket so he could make proper teas for the rest of the week. That took the wind out of her sails!

Mum looked at the shopping list Dad had printed off for her. She peeped under the plate-cover.

'Well...this is incredible,' she goes. 'And on a Monday too, your busiest day.'

Dad stopped trying to stick the chimney on. He had forgotten all about his match reports! He grabbed his notes and laptop and dashed off up to his study.

As Dad opened the door to the stairs we clearly heard the sound of Primrose sobbing on the settee. I told Mum she had been like that on and off since we got home from school. Matt must have finished with her.

Mum looked worried. After Mushy Marcus finished with Primrose she had got stuck in the wailing stage for weeks.

'I tried to talk to her,' I said, 'but she told me to go away.'

I followed Mum upstairs. She perched on the end of the settee until Primrose shifted her legs and let her sit down properly.

'Are you all right, honey-bun?' said Mum, stroking her leg.

'No-o-o-o!' Primrose wailed. 'Oh, Mum – Matt doesn't want to go out with me any more!'

She sat up and pitched forwards, burying her face in Mum's shoulder.

'Did he send you a text?' asked Mum, giving her a hug.

Primrose felt around on the cushions behind her and found her phone. She brought Matt's message up on the screen. Mum read it.

'But Primrose darling,' she said. 'All he says here is that he wants to cool things for a while.'

'That's what people always say when they want to end it!'

'Maybe you're right, but I don't think they normally add, "Let's talk about everything when the exams are over."'

'He's just trying to let me down gently!'

Mum said had it occurred to Primrose that Matt might mean exactly what he said? He was a bright young man; he would want to work hard and do well.

'He'd want a girlfriend who works hard and does well too,' she said. 'Look, he says, "Good luck in your exams."'

'O-o-o-oh!' Primrose let out another great wail. 'I've been stupid, I've been a pain! He did want to go out with me and now I've driven him away!'

There was no arguing with that. But Mum said of course she wasn't stupid; she had just got really stressed about exams and Matt would understand that.

'No-o-o-o-o! It isn't just exams – I'm always like this. I hate myself!' cried Primrose.

At that point Mum said that possibly, perhaps, sometimes Primrose might be just a little teeny tiny bit highly-strung...but there was really nothing wrong with that.

I don't know whether it was Mum's pep talk, or the thought that Matt would prefer a clever girlfriend, or the fact that after all this build-up Primrose had her first actual exam the following day, but she did stop crying eventually. She went upstairs to wash her face and do some revision.

Mum sat back with a sigh. 'Poor Primrose. She really does make life hard for herself.'

'She shouldn't be such a drama queen.'

'I don't suppose she wants to be so stormy,' Mum said. 'I should think she'd much rather be sunny and settled like you.'

That made me feel cross. Just because I didn't thrash around making a big fuss about the slightest thing, that didn't mean I was always sunny inside. Right now, for example, I was definitely overcast.

Mum didn't seem to notice. 'Maybe your sister needs a bit more Mum-time,' she sighed. 'I've let my work get out of hand, when here she is in the middle of exams and struggling with her love-life too.'

This made me even more cross. What about me and Dad? I didn't say anything, though.

'It's hard starting up your own business,' Mum said, 'but you have to keep a grip on the things that really matter. Maybe Stella wouldn't mind doing more than half the work for the time being, as her children have all grown up and left home.'

Suddenly, we heard a huge crash from the kitchen. There was nobody down there but Dennis. We ran downstairs to find out what had happened. His mighty mansion was lying on its side and Dennis was sticking up out of the window, trying to wriggle out.

Mum pointed out that Dennis was a heavy rabbit and his house was tall and light. Therefore, if he made it to the top floor, the whole thing would obviously be unstable. She got hold of him under the armpits and hauled him out. He looked too startled to try and bite her.

'See, Dennis is another reason I need to cut back on my work,' goes Mum. 'Look what happened because I was too busy to check the safety measures you lot put in place – he nearly died. What's more, he could have burnt the house down! We've all got to be a lot more careful with him from now on.'

'S-so – Dennis doesn't have to go?'

'No,' said Mum, 'it's far too late for that.' She put him down on the floor. 'He might be a proper little nuisance but he's a member of the family now. We're stuck with him.'

So Gran was officially a genius. Things had worked out exactly as she had said – all we had to do was hold on to Dennis for a few weeks, and now everyone was so used to having him around, there was no question of letting him go.

What's more, although it was hard to see how it had happened, I couldn't help noticing that right now Primrose was upstairs revising, Mum was working out how to cut down her hours, and Dad had proper meals planned for the whole week. Could that be, in some weird way, down to Dennis? You had to wonder.

Chapter 15
Losing Someone you Love and Getting your Head Blown Off

Dad and me converted Dennis's mansion into a bungalow. Mum said on the upside it meant he wouldn't break his neck jumping around in there, but on the downside it took up three times as much of the floor.

I was trying to teach Dennis some tricks before the weekend to show Gran because she had managed to get a few days off to come and visit.

You and Your Rabbit was not encouraging. It said rabbits weren't famous for their brain-power and it would take a particularly clever one a whole lifetime to learn to recognise its own name.

Dennis was turning out to be an Einstein of the rabbit world, in that case. He definitely looked up when I said his name, and he more than looked up when he heard the sound of a biscuit breaking or a slice of toast popping up. He came and sat on your feet until you gave him some.

Before long, I had taught him to beg by holding a piece of food just too high for him to reach. You had to give it to him as soon as he was up on his hind legs, though, or else he'd drop back down on all fours, turn his back on you and sulk.

I wished I could train him to let me pick him up. I still had to grab him from above because if he saw me coming he would thump his foot and try to nip me. Once I had got him he would only stay on my knee for a few seconds before he hopped off, shaking his bottom like someone who's sat on a garden chair with a puddle of rainwater on it.

But although Dennis wasn't exactly cuddly, he had at least stopped going for Primrose all the time. He tried to chase her once or twice but when she didn't react in the usual way by getting stroppy and making a lot of noise he didn't seem to know what to do.

Primrose had gone all quiet and droopy. It was partly because she had exams every day that week, but it was mostly because she was convinced it was over with Matt, whatever he'd said exactly. 'I really loved him,' she told me one day. 'And now I've lost him.'

I tried to imagine how it must feel to be like Primrose, one minute all fired up and angry and the next minute all fizzled-out and sad. I felt sorry for her, even though she was nuts to give up on Matt when she really didn't have to.

I knew what it felt like to lose someone you really loved. I remembered what it had felt like losing Sam – I still missed taking him for our walks even though I had Dennis now. I couldn't bear to think how I would feel if I was ever to lose Dennis.

The weather had turned baking hot. 'Typical,' Primrose said. 'It's always sunny when I've got exams.' The sky was bright blue and the sun sparkled on the sea. The town was full of tourists. Some people call them emmets, which means ants, but they were more like snails now we had a heat-wave, moving super-slowly under their sun-hats and shades.

I was going super-slowly too, as I walked down the zig-zag path on Friday after school. All the doors and windows along the terrace were open and you could hear sounds of music and chatting from inside.

Dad was at the table reading the paper. He had both the front and back doors open to try and get a bit of a breeze. Dennis was lying in the sunny patch under the radiator, dozing. Rabbits don't usually do that according to You and Your Rabbit. They don't completely go to sleep because they might get grabbed by a passing fox or cat. Or someone picking them up from above, I guess.

It seemed a shame to disturb him so I went upstairs to change out of my school uniform first. Primrose was lying on the settee watching TV. She had done her last exam now so she wasn't stressing about her revision; she was stressing about her results instead. The sitting room's got a huge window so it was quite cool in there and I decided to hang around for a while.

We must have both dozed off – two million degrees of heat plus The Story of Coal Mining on the History Channel can do that to you. I have no idea why we were watching that.

Anyway, what woke us was Dad hollering up the stairs at us.

'Dennis has disappeared!'

We ran downstairs. Dad was in a right state.

'I dropped my biscuit on the floor and he didn't

come and grab it,' he said. 'You know what he's like. I thought there must be something wrong with him. I've searched high and low but I can't find him!'

'He'll be out in the yard,' Primrose said. We didn't bother with the barrier on the back door any more because we thought he'd never be able to get out of the yard, the walls were too high. 'Have you looked behind the pots?'

Dad said of course he had looked behind the pots, and under the sun loungers and everywhere else. Dennis was definitely not in the yard.

'He must be in his bungalow,' I said, lifting one end up. But it was too light. No Dennis in there.

We all looked at the barrier across the front door. Was it possible he could have jumped over it? He wasn't a very athletic sort of rabbit, but on the other hand it wasn't a very big barrier.

We stepped over it onto the wide top step, which is more like a balcony really, with the stairs going sideways down the wall from the door. There used to be a pot of geraniums in one corner but it looked as if someone had come along and snipped all the flowers and leaves off with some scissors. Now it was just a pot of stalks.

Beside the base of the pot there was a cluster of little round poos. We saw one or two more on the steps, but then the trail ran out. We knew he had got past the barrier but it was impossible to tell which way up or down the zig-zag path Dennis had gone.

'Well, that's it,' said Primrose. 'We've lost him.'

I glared at her.

'He's a rabbit,' she said. 'Running and hiding are the things he does best. Get real, Peony, we're never going to find him, are we?'

'We've got to find him!' I said, looking frantically up and down the path.

'He can't have been gone more than a few minutes,' said Dad.

Primrose said there was no need to worry about Dennis. He would be all right. He would like being free. He would find some wild rabbits to live with and have a lovely life.

'Don't be stupid!' I cried. 'He'll never survive in the wild. He's grey and white! Foxes and dogs will see him a mile off, and wild rabbits won't have anything to do with him. They'll think he's weird! And anyway, this isn't the wild, it's Polgotherick! There are cars and buses and...and... What if he falls in the sea?'

I started to shake. It felt as if I had an engine vibrating inside me. I couldn't stop it. It must have looked as bad as it felt because Primrose said, 'Stop it, Peony! You're freaking me out!'

'I c-c-can't lose him, Primrose.'

Dad said, 'I'll search down towards the town, Primrose can search up towards the top road and Peony, you knock on some doors and ask if anyone's seen him.'

'That's no good, it'll take too long,' said Primrose. 'He'll be half-way to Truro before we've searched the terrace.'

She opened her mouth and let out the loudest shout I had ever heard.

'HE-E-E-LP!'

It was a shout that could blow your head off. It shocked the shakes right out of me and left me standing there, gawping like a goldfish.

Chapter 16
A Scary Scream and a Surprising Skill

'What are you *doing*?'

Primrose ignored me.

'Help! Help!' she yelled at the top of her lungs.

Mr Kaminski burst out of his house brandishing a broom. Dad had his back to him and he must have thought he was a strange man attacking Primrose. He surged down the steps and would have hit Dad over the head with his broom if he hadn't turned round in the nick of time.

'Dave!' Mr Kaminski stopped in his tracks. 'Is problem?'

'We've lost Dennis,' said Dad.

'Is that your rabbit?' asked Mrs Robertson from number 5. All the neighbours were coming out to see what was going on. From the top of his ladder, the man mending the gutters at number 7 called over, 'Is he a big fellow? White?'

Everyone turned to look up at him.

'Have you seen him?' asked Dad.

'I reckon I might have,' said the man. 'Just out of the corner of my eye, like. I thought he was a funny-looking cat.'

'Which way did he go?'

The man pointed up the path. There was no sign of Dennis but Mum had just turned the bend and was haring down the hill towards us. She nearly crashed into a family in beach shorts who had strolled onto the path from the grassy track that leads out towards Nash House and the cliffs. They speeded up and followed her to find out what was going on.

'What's wrong?' called Mum. She must have heard Primrose yelling all the way up at the Medical Centre where she was doing the hanging baskets.

'Dennis has disappeared,' said Dad. 'That chap up the ladder said he saw him going up the hill.'

'He isn't on the path,' said Mum. 'I would have seen him.'

'He must have got all the way to the road then,' I cried. 'He'll get run over!'

'Unless he went onto the coastal path,' suggested the woman in the beach shorts. 'We didn't see him, but he could be anywhere up there amongst the gorse and bracken.'

Everyone offered to help us search. Some people said they would go to the top and look around near the road and in the fields on the far side. Some people said they would take the coastal path and search the cliffs.

Just as we were heading up the hill we heard a shout behind us. It was Matt. He had heard Primrose screaming for help and run all the way up from the beach with two of his mates.

'Are you alright?' he gasped. He looked really worried.

Primrose explained about Dennis going missing, and how we needed a search party quick-smart because we'd never find him on our own. Anyone else might have felt annoyed about being hauled off from the beach when it wasn't a matter of life or death, but Matt was such an animal-lover he totally got it.

'We'll help,' he said. 'This is Jonno and Squid.'

We all strode up the hill until we came to

the place where the coast path split off. Then Primrose, Matt and his mates went on up to the road with Mr Kaminski, Mrs Robertson, James and Cath from number 11, the man who was mending the gutter and two ladies in sunhats who happened to be passing by.

Me, Mum, Dad, Mr Adlin from number 4, the beach-shorts family and Mrs Stubbs from the shop went over the stile onto the grassy path towards the cliffs. Some woman who was walking her dog came to help us too.

Our group got as far as Nash House and then stopped. There was nothing ahead except miles and miles of bracken and gorse. It just seemed hopeless. But Mrs Robertson said we couldn't give up. Dennis was big, he was mostly white, and if he was out here we had an excellent chance of spotting him.

The band of neighbours and passers-by fanned out from the path and began searching through the undergrowth. Me, Mum and Dad stood by the boarded-up gate of Nash House. Mum squeezed my hand. She must have guessed what I was thinking.

Dad said, 'There's no chance Dennis could have gone into Nash House is there? I mean, this wall does go all the way round?'

Mum said it did. But then she suddenly

remembered there was one place on the far side of the house where a tree had grown against the wall and pushed it in. The stones had shifted and made a narrow split.

'But it's *very* narrow,' she said. 'I don't think Dennis could get through.'

'He did squeeze through the gap beside the fridge,' Dad pointed out.

'Oh!' gasped Mum. 'I've just remembered what's on the other side of that bit of wall. An old herb garden with a massive patch of parsley!'

Dennis would squeeze through a pinhole to get at some parsley – it was his favourite food in the world. If he had got a whiff of it on his travels out towards the cliffs he would definitely have made a diversion.

There were big brambles and nettles growing against the wall but we pushed our way through. Even Dad couldn't see over the top because it was so high. We came to the corner.

As we picked our way along the back of the wall we heard a terrible sound. It was frightening, high, eerie; it was like nothing I had ever heard before.

We stopped and stared at each other. I had read in You and Your Rabbit that rabbits can scream. 'A rabbit's scream is a sound you would never want to hear,' it said. I wished I never had heard it.

Dad set off again, faster now, with Mum and me close behind. We could see the tree up ahead. It was stunted and thorny, leaning into the wall like a ragged old witch. When we reached it we saw the crack. It was barely wider than my arm and it ran right down the wall.

I pushed my face up to it and peered through. I could see the edge of the parsley patch, a bit of brick path, a broken wheelbarrow. There was no sign of Dennis. But then I caught sight of something that made my blood run cold. Hidden in a patch of long grass, still as stone, there was a big brown cat.

The cat's yellow eyes were fixed on a spot to one side of the crack, and I knew that was where Dennis must be. But the wall was so thick and the crack was so narrow, we would never be able to get to him. I started to shake again, even worse than before.

Mum and Dad were looking through the crack higher up. 'W-w-what are we g-g-going to do?' I whispered. I didn't want to alarm Dennis because if he tried to make a dash for it, the cat would pounce.

I thought Mum would know what to do – she always knew. But she looked as lost as me. She tried to pull me away from the wall. I knew she didn't want me to see what would happen next.

All of a sudden, Dad leapt into action. He grabbed some stones that had fallen out of the wall and shinned straight up the tree. His feet were higher than my head before I realised what was happening. Me and Mum looked at each other in astonishment.

Dad got a toe-hold high on the wall and heaved himself up to the top. We peered through the gap again and saw the cat glaring up at Dad. It didn't look scared, just cross, and it wasn't moving.

Dad threw a stone at it. It was a great shot. It flew through the air like a deadly missile and would have hit the cat right between the eyes if it hadn't jumped out of the way.

We heard a thump behind the wall and a rustle of leaves and suddenly Dennis appeared in the gap. His eyes were wide open and his nose was going nuts. He pushed himself into the crack and tried to wriggle through. He wriggled and wriggled but the gap was too tight.

The cat saw Dennis was trying to escape. It leapt at him. I screamed – and with a mighty roar, Dad jumped down off the wall. Thump! The cat stopped in its tracks. Its yellow eyes flashed in anger but it stood its ground,

Dad ran at the cat, yelling and waving his arms, and it saw he meant business. It yowled and dived back into the long grass, with Dad on its tail. We saw them race away across the garden and disappear out of sight.

Dennis, wriggling like fury, finally managed to squeeze his way out of the crack. I thought he would try to get away but he just stood there looking up at me. I picked him up and held on to him.

'Small problem,' gasped Dad, arriving back on the other side of the wall. 'How am I going to get back over?'

Mum laughed. She said she had seen an old step-ladder in the potting-shed. Five minutes later, Dad appeared at the top of the wall. He scrambled back down the tree. He was covered in scratches and had twigs and leaves in his hair.

Mum grinned at him. She gave him a big hug.

I said, 'I didn't know you could climb trees, Dad!'

Dad kissed Mum's cheek and smiled at me over her shoulder.

'I used to be a champion scrumper in my young days, I'll have you know.'

I suddenly imagined my dad as a boy, out scrumping for apples and plums with his friends. Fishing, crabbing, playing hide-and-seek in the bracken.

'It's surprising what skills you can pick up just messing around!' he said.

Mum called everyone over. They were delighted that we'd found Dennis. Some of them tried to stroke him, and he nestled deeper into my arms as if he was backing into a burrow.

Dad called Primrose on his mobile. 'We've found him...up at Nash House...yes... Say thank you to everyone up there for us...'

When we finally got home I put Dennis down near his hutch. I expected him to hop up and hide in the bedroom end for a while. But he put his front paws on my leg and looked up at me as if to say, 'Don't put me down! I need another cuddle!'

Chapter 17
The Friends you Choose and the Family you Want

It was Saturday afternoon and Gran was coming for supper. She said she had some news for us. That was always slightly worrying. If her old bones were fed up with surfing, maybe she had decided to take off on a round-the-world trip or be a bird warden or go and teach English in Africa.

Mum was cooking beetroot lasagne. It looks worse than it tastes because the beetroot turns everything red, but that's not saying much. Beetroot is bad enough cold with salad – no-one should have to eat it hot.

Still, Mum was happy. At least we would be getting some proper meals again now, she said. She had talked to Stella about cutting down on her work and it turned out Stella's son was home from university for the summer and couldn't find a job, so he was dead keen to take over half Mum's lawns and hedges.

Dad was making a better barrier for the front door. It was like a gate across the bottom half, made of chicken-wire on a wooden frame. It was too high to step over so you had to open and shut it, but at least it meant we could leave the front door open to get a bit of air through and not have to worry about Dennis going walkabout.

Dennis was in his house happily munching out a new window. There were lots of holes in it now and he would stick his head through one and then another, nibbling them bigger. Dad said it reminded him of Squeaky, the little mouse he found in the garden shed when he was a boy. He kept it in a shoe-box until it chewed a hole in the side and ran away. We've learnt a lot of things about Dad since we got Dennis.

Primrose was doing her nails at the kitchen table 'just in case'. Look how quickly Matt had come running when he heard her shout for help, she said. There was only one explanation for that: he must still like her.

Just as Dad was ready to test his new safety gate, Gran arrived. Mum was putting the lasagne in the oven. 'What perfect timing!' she said. Primrose was blowing on her nails and Dennis had just discovered his window was finally big enough to stick his whole head through.

'What's with the new barrier?' asked Gran, carefully hooking it shut after her. We had half an hour before supper to tell her the story of Dennis's great adventure and the massive search operation we had to organise to get him back.

Dennis came out of his house to sniff Gran's toes. I wondered if he knew we were talking about him. It didn't seem likely. The more you got to know Dennis, the more you had to think maybe the book was right. Rabbits were gorgeous, funny and sweet, plus they were fully house-trainable. But they didn't understand things, like a dog. Sam would definitely know if you were talking about him.

I felt bad about having those kinds of thoughts so I picked Dennis up and gave him a cuddle, which he seemed to like now. He wasn't the same as Sam but he was lovely in his own way. Gran reached over and stroked him.

'He must have been so scared,' she said. 'Thank goodness you managed to find him.'

While we were setting the table Gran asked Mum about the garden up at Nash House.

'They've offered me the job if I want it,' said Mum. 'But I don't know...'

'What's the problem?'

'Well they want to lose all the lovely old features like the brick paths and out-buildings and lay lots of gravel. They reckon that's what buyers are looking for. They're probably going to do something similar with the house.'

Mum took the lasagne out the oven and put it proudly on the mat in the middle of the table. It was bubbling hot and bright purple. Gran obviously hadn't seen a beetroot lasagne before because she nearly passed out in surprise.

'Are you feeling all right, Gran?' asked Primrose.

Mum said it was probably the shock of hearing what they were going to do to Nash House.

'Someone should make them an offer for it just as it is,' she said. 'Then they could do it up the way they want to, which hopefully wouldn't mean covering the whole place with concrete and gravel.'

'You know what?' goes Gran. 'I might just do that!'

We all gawped at her.

'That's my news,' she said. 'I've handed in my notice and I'm moving back to Polgotherick!'

Before anyone had a chance to say anything, Mr Kaminski appeared at the front door looking very smart. His hair was combed back and he was wearing a brand new cardigan.

'Hello, hello – is good time to call?'

'Of course,' said Mum. 'Come in and have some supper.'

'Aaah...' sighed Mr K, sniffing the air. 'Is beetroot, yes?'

He must be the only person in the universe except Mum who actually likes beetroot. She laid an extra place between Primrose and Gran.

'My mother's just told us she's moving back to Polgotherick,' said Dad.

Mr Kaminski's face lit up. 'Is wonderful news!' he exclaimed.

'Well, it's all to do with a new job I've got in mind,' goes Gran. I knew it wasn't just about giving up the surf school!

'I'm thinking of getting my skipper's certificate and doing boat trips round the harbour,' she said.

This seemed like a surprisingly good idea, so we all nodded encouragingly. But it's not good to be too encouraging when Gran gets an idea, because sometimes it means she straight away has another one.

'You're a sea-faring man, Viktor,' she said. 'Why don't you come in with me?'

Dad looked worried. 'Just as long as he'll still have time for the problem page.'

'Ah, yes, the problem page,' goes Gran. 'I'd forgotten about that. How's it going now, Viktor? Did you tell them the family that plays together stays together, like I said? That's why I got Dennis for this little family here.'

Mum and Dad looked astonished.

'Well, you did all seem to be a bit...stressed,' mumbled Gran.

Luckily for her, at that very minute we heard someone coming up the front steps. It was Matt.

'I just came to see how Dennis is doing,' he said.

'How nice!' goes Mum. 'Come in and have some pudding.'

Pudding was Mum's famous rhubarb upside-down cake, where you take a perfectly nice cake and float it on a stringy soup of revolting rhubarb. Bad timing, Matt!

Sam stood huffing behind the safety gate. You could tell he was getting a whiff of something much more interesting than rhubarb.

'Will Dennis be all right with Sam?' Matt asked.

'I should think so,' said Mum, 'but it might be best if he stays outside until after we've eaten.'

Matt left Sam on the front step and came inside. He squeezed in next to Primrose.

'You were awesome when Dennis went missing,' he said to her. 'Shouting out like that, getting everyone together, organising the search. You were amazing.'

Primrose did a sort of sob of joy and flung herself at him. He caught her like some giant floppy beach-ball and held on. It looked like Matt was back.

Matt and Primrose sat beaming at each other while Mum turned the rhubarb upside-down cake out onto a big plate and Dad microwaved the custard.

You can choose your friends, Gran said, it's just your family you're stuck with. Matt had a chance to stay away from Primrose but he chose to come back. It was a bit mysterious, but brilliant, especially as we might need someone to help pick up the pieces when the exam results came out.

After supper Matt let Sam in. Dennis shot into his house and wouldn't come out. He kept thumping his feet, making the boxes rattle.

'Lie down, Sam,' said Matt. Sam lay down and I sat beside him, stroking his wiry old fur. After about five hundred hours Dennis finally plucked up the courage to peep out of one of his windows.

Sam's nose twitched and his ears went up.

'Stay,' said Matt. 'Good boy.'

Dennis crept out of his front door, flattening his body to the floor. He stood stock still, staring at Sam.

'This is Sam,' I told him. I put one hand on Sam's back and held the other one out towards Dennis. Dennis came to sniff my fingers. He sniffed all the way along my arm. Then he started sniffing Sam. Sam kept completely still, looking up at Matt.

See, that's the thing about Sam. He's clever. He understands. He knows what you want him to do, not like Dennis who's adorable but dizzy. They were chalk and cheese, like Jess and Toby at school when you came to think about it – Jess so brainy and Toby so practical. I didn't love one more than the other – I wanted them both.

Dennis was getting bolder. He sniffed all the way along Sam's side. He started to nibble his fur! Sam was giving Matt his do-I-really-have-to-put-up-with-this? look.

Matt gave Sam the slightest little nod and Sam stood up. Dennis froze. It's what rabbits do, because they think if they keep completely still you can't see them. Of course, it works better with brown rabbits in the wild.

Sam sniffed him. He prodded him with his nose. Then he sat down again.

'They're going to be friends,' said Matt.

Later, I took Sam for a walk. The sun was going down over the sea but the air was still warm. I stood at the top of the steps while he slowly worked his way down. Then we set off towards the harbour together.

Sam stopped every five seconds to have a sniff around and that meant I had to slow down too. I started to notice things; the petals falling off the roses outside Crab Apple Cottage, two cigarette ends wedged between the cobbles, a spider's web shuddering in a gateway.

When you walk with Sam you don't only start to notice things – you start to think about things too. I thought about the wishes I had written down on my piece of paper. I remembered Gran saying those were the kind of wishes that won't work. I had felt so fed up when she said that, but now I was glad.

If Dad hadn't been lazing around reading his paper, scoffing and dropping his biscuit, no-one would have noticed Dennis was missing. And if he hadn't wasted so much time messing around when he was a boy he would never have learnt how to throw stones and shin up trees and jump down off eight-foot walls. A lazy old lion might sleep most of the day, but watch out when he springs into action!

If Primrose hadn't been such a drama queen

she would have been too embarrassed, like me, to shout out at the top of her lungs and make everyone come running. We would have knocked on doors and politely asked passers-by if they had seen him, and then we wouldn't have got to him in time, before the cat closed in.

If Mum hadn't been working her socks off cutting grass all over Polgotherick the people selling Nash House wouldn't have heard of Garden Angels and then none of us would have known about the gap in the wall and the parsley on the other side.

And if Gran wasn't an ideas person we would never have got Dennis.

'It's a surprising thing,' I said to Sam, as we sat down on the harbour wall. 'But I suddenly do feel happy to have the family I've got.'

I'm sure he understood.

Will Gran move back to Polgotherick? Will Mr Kaminski still have time to help Dad with the problem page? And will Peony still choose Toby and Jess when the cool kids at school want to be her friends? Find out what happens next in:

How to Get the Friends You Want
by Peony Pinker

ISBN 9781408152362

Read on for a sneak preview...

Chapter 1
Dad on Breakfast-time TV
and Dennis's Mad Dash

You know when something exciting happens first thing in the morning and you just can't wait to get to school and tell your friends?

But then your rabbit, Dennis, kicks orange juice all over your big sister's school bag and she gets in a bad mood and says, 'What friends?'

Well, that's what happened to me the day that Dad got on breakfast-time TV.

It was still dark outside when I woke up but there was a strip of light under the door so I knew someone else was already up. It couldn't be Primrose because she's as sluggish as a sloth first thing in the morning. I read about sloths in 'Animals of the World'. They move so slowly they actually get moss growing on them – true story.

I put my dressing-gown and slippers on and went downstairs. There was no-one in the sitting room, which is on the floor below my and Primrose's bedrooms, so I went on down the next flight of stairs to the kitchen. All the houses in

Harbour Row are very tall and thin.

Mum was sitting at the table eating a slice of toast.

'You're up nice and early,' she said. 'Well I suppose it isn't every day a person's dad gets on breakfast-time TV!'

She got up to put some more toast on. 'I just hope he makes it... You know what he's like.'

One of Dad's favourite mottoes is, 'Better late than having to set the alarm,' so the chance of him getting to the studios by 7 o'clock wasn't high. I was actually half hoping he wouldn't manage it because, under the circumstances, he would almost certainly make a fool of himself if he did.

'I'd better wake Primrose up,' Mum said, glancing at the clock. 'She'd hate to miss it.'

She went off upstairs and I gave Dennis a corner of my toast. Rabbits are supposed to like lettuce and leaves but he prefers bread and biscuits. Maybe it's an indoor-rabbit thing.

When Mum came back down she made some tea and we took it upstairs to the sitting room to drink in front of the TV. We shut the stair gate so Dennis couldn't come up. He mostly lives in the kitchen because it's one hundred percent rabbit-proof, unlike the rest of the house. Dad's made gates across the front and back doors as well as the stairs, to keep him in.

The book says rabbits are fully house-trainable, which is true. What the book doesn't tell you is that your fully-house-trained rabbit is like a chewing machine. He'll nibble through anything he can get to – furniture, wires, floor coverings, door frames. He'll even nibble the plaster off the corners of your walls. It's like those giant ants on David Attenborough that march into your house and munch their way through until there's nothing left but a few sticks and a pile of rubble. I'm not saying Dennis has got that far yet, but he's definitely working on it.

'Primrose!' Mum yelled up to her again as there still wasn't any sound of movement from her bedroom. 'It's going to be on any minute!'

There was a crash and a loud groan, followed by a grumble. A slow th...ump-th...ump on the stairs, and about fifty hours later, Primrose appeared. Her eyes were half-closed and her hair was all over the place.

'W-what's going on?'

'Dad's on breakfast time TV – remember?' said Mum.

'Oh, yeah,' goes Primrose. 'Have I got time to get some breakfast?'

'If you're quick.'

Primrose quick? Fat chance! She staggered down to the kitchen, mumbling and rubbing her eyes. We heard her fumbling around. The programme started with some clips of what was coming up. Dad hadn't only got there in time – he was going to be the first one on the sofa.

Mum called down to Primrose that she'd better hurry up or she would miss it.

'Our first guest this morning is Dave Pinker, the man behind the Dear Daphne page on the Three Towns Gazette. Dave was last night voted Best Agony Aunt of the Year at the prestigious Association of Agony Aunts Annual Presentation Dinner!'

Primrose arrived just in time as the camera panned across to Dad. She had a bowl of cereal in one hand and a glass of orange juice in the other. She put the orange juice on the floor by her feet so she could eat the cereal once she had geared herself up to it. Like I said, in the mornings Primrose is slo-o-o-o-w.

'So, Dave,' said the presenter. 'Congratulations on winning this award. What, would you say, is the secret of being a great agony aunt?'

'I don't really know,' Dad said, with a modest shrug.

It was true – he didn't have a clue.

And don't miss Peony's first hilarious outing...

How to Get What You Want
by Peony Pinker

Peony wants a lot of things. She wants a dog,
she wants her dad to stop being the world's
worst agony aunt, and she really wants to get rid
of Primrose's horrible best friend Bianca. Then
Mr Kaminski next door tells her the secret of
how to get what you want, and Peony decides
it's time to put a stop to Bianca at last.

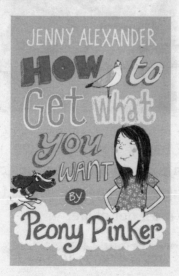

ISBN 9781408132876

Also by Jenny Alexander:

How 2B Happy :-)

Get the happy habit! Bursting with funny stories, things to do and great advice, this is a brilliant book for anyone who wants to feel good and get the most out of life.

ISBN 9780713675597